# FESTIVAL OF SOULS

# Festival of Souls

## *a Jen Rice novel*

SHANON L. MAYER

Shanon L. Mayer

First Printing, 2023

Cover design by JD&J Design

ISBN (Paperback): 9781958076002
ISBN (eBook): 9781958076019

Published by Shanon L. Mayer, Vancouver WA 98663
https://shanonlmayer.com

For Beau. You will never be forgotten.

# Books by Shanon L. Mayer

# Chapter 1

The moon rose, full and swollen, over the trees. As Jen Rice watched through the narrow window, she waited for the sensation of change, for the pain to wash over her body, for the claws and teeth to push through her skin as her bones bent into new, unfamiliar shapes. The window was relatively high, but from her height of just under five ten she was able to see the treetops that marked the edge of the horizon. The moon was bright and appeared far too cheerful for her taste, considering what she was about to endure. She pushed a strand of hair, so dark it was almost as black as the shadows that surrounded her, and watched the moon as it slowly inched into the sky, waiting for fur to grow over her body and a tail to spring from the base of her spine. She waited for the moon to do its worst.

The back of her left shoulder burned where the werewolf's claws had torn through her skin, possibly passing its infection to her and causing her to stand at the window, behind solid bars, waiting to turn into a monster. A single tear slipped from her eye as she felt a tingle course through her body and she fell onto the mattress on the floor, waiting.

All around her, she could hear other Weres, every bit as captive as she, howling as they shifted from their human form to their canine bodies. Pain, excitement, even relief echoed in their screams, and Jen squeezed her eyes closed to block out as much of it as she could.

Fifteen minutes later, she opened her dark brown eyes, ever so slightly, to look at the moon. The very top edge of it shone in through her window, visible from the cold, hard mattress on the floor. For it to be that high, it certainly had to be fully risen. She opened her eyes the rest of the way, sat up, and looked around. The door was solid metal but there was a small window set high up and a scattering of holes had been carefully and strategically placed in the upper half of the door as well. The concrete floor and cinderblock walls muffled a lot of the noise from the Weres that she knew were shifting all around her but seemed to reflect the sounds as well, causing an eerie echo. Other noises reverberated through the walls to mix with the werewolf cries, such as the murmurs of conversation from the doctors, nurses, security, volunteers, and other staff of North Bank Hospital, where she was currently a guest of the lunar wing.

Since she was locked in for the night, whether she changed or not, she sighed and settled back onto the mattress, pulling the thin wool blanket up over her shoulders to try and get some sleep. The six-foot-long blanket wasn't quite long enough for her to be comfortable beneath but at least she wasn't very wide. The extra workouts she had been subjected to as a part of her new employment had added a small amount of muscle to her already lean frame but she was still shaped more like her brother than like her sisters. She brushed a wisp of black hair off of her forehead and tried to settle down.

Gradually, the howls of werewolves faded into the growls and grumbles of their feeding time and Jen tried not to consider how many of them preferred their meat alive. When she was headed into the hospital to check in, she had seen how many animals were brought in for just this occasion and she doubted that any would be left tomorrow. In the morning, if she was still curious, she could ask her friend Joel.

Just as she was drifting into sleep, she heard shouting and a commotion in the hall outside her cell. Immediately alert, she popped to her feet and scurried to see what was going on. She stretched up onto her toes to be able to see through the window that was set into the door but still wasn't able to see much. The thick plastic obscured most of her visibility, not that her angle was useful to begin with. What she could see, however, was that a handful of people were rushing about, a lot more hurried than normal. Shouting, louder than the rest of the ruckus, filtered through the thick plexiglass but she couldn't tell what was being said among all the other yelling.

When a sound that very much resembled a

gunshot echoed through the door, she ducked below the reinforced steel, wishing she had at been allowed to keep least one of her weapons with her. It hadn't seemed necessary to ask whether the plexiglass was bulletproof when she had initially been taken into the cell, which suddenly felt like a tremendous oversight on her part. The commotion outside increased for just a moment before calming and by the time Jen felt safe enough to attempt to see what had happened again, everything appeared to be back to normal. After watching for a couple more minutes, she decided that whatever had been going on was over and headed back to her mattress.

Early in the morning, she was woken again by werewolf howls. This time, instead of starting as human cries that turned canine, these were wolf howls that faded into human whimpering as the imprisoned werewolves transformed into humans once more. Hearing this, Jen knew that her release was imminent so she quickly changed out of the scrubs she had been given and back into her comfortable jeans, hooded long-sleeved shirt, and sneakers. Unsure of what was expected under her particular circumstances, she folded the scrubs and sat on the mattress, waiting to be let out.

She hadn't expected her release to come as quickly as it did, nor in the manner in which it came. Instead of Joel Peters, her longtime friend and volunteer at the hospital who had brought her in the previous night, her door was opened and unlocked by Marc Anderson, her unit leader in New World Response. His leg was still in a cast from being broken a short time ago and he didn't look pleased to be out walking on it now. He tossed her gear bag in to her and closed the door again before she had a chance to catch the bag. "Gear up," he called in through the door.

Confused and more than a little curious, she changed into her battle gear. First was her armor, thick layers of canvas and heavy leather with thin silver wires woven between them. Next, she put on her uniform, black pants and shirt, both with lots of pockets. Finally, she stepped into her boots and buckled on her duty belt, slipping her pistol, taser, and pair of spray canisters into their holders on the belt. When she was ready, she banged on the door and shouldered the strap to her rifle. "I'm ready."

Although she was the newest member of the New World Response unit, Jen had more than earned her place in the group. After a short time of trying to get to know each other, she and the rest of her team had finally settled into an understanding. Because of that, she didn't question why they were there to pick her up, she simply stepped out the door and followed.

To her surprise, Troy, Joel's best friend and Jen's part-time protector, was there as well. He was a bit taller than her, with shaggy brown hair and a week's worth of growth on his chin. He wasn't a member of the response team, so she wasn't sure why he would have been brought down to get her if they were rolling out on a mission. She shot a questioning glance at him as they walked through the hospital's corridors, but he refused to respond, instead keeping a watchful eye out around them and holding his own rifle at the ready.

Finally, she spoke up. "Where are we going?"

"We're taking you home," A voice answered from behind her. She whipped around to discover a tall, red-haired man with a scattering of freckles across his nose and bright green eyes. "Patrick?" she asked as she recognized her older brother. "What are you doing here, too?"

"Helping to keep you safe, of course. Come on, let's go."

As they walked through the hospital halls, Jen noticed that there was a lot more security on guard than there had been when she had walked in. The previous night, she had only seen a scant handful of the hospital's response team but there were dozens walking the halls now. While most of them ignored the New World team as they walked through, a few turned to look curiously at Jen as they passed. "Will someone tell me what's going on?"

"Later," Marc answered her. "Once we get you home, I'll tell you what I know. For right now, I just want to get you out of here." He shot a glance over his shoulder as they reached the doors that led outside. "Did you shift?"

She shook her head. "No."

He nodded and held the door for her. "Good to know."

"Would it have mattered if I did?" she asked

as she walked through the door. She had been wanting to ask that question the entire time since being attacked by a werewolf, the possibility of infection high, but had been afraid to know the answer. Safe from shapeshifting for the moment, curiosity won.

"Only on a full moon," responded another member of the unit, this one with bright blue eyes, far too much tan than was natural at the end of autumn, and a goatee that almost reached his collar. To Jen, Mike Brown's goatee looked like a goat's beard, although there was no way she would ever tell him that directly.

Walking next to Mike was J.J. Monroe, half a foot taller than Jen, with curly blond hair and pale blue eyes. They were followed by Ty Williams, the tallest of the group, who had skin the color of coffee and, Jen was certain, no body hair whatsoever. She hadn't figured out yet whether he naturally didn't grow hair or if he kept it shaved. Right then, however, he was busily watching out behind them and waiting for the rest of the group to head out the doors into the parking garage.

The unit's trucks were parked just outside

the door in an area reserved for response vehicles. Since Jen had ridden with Joel on the way in to the hospital, her emerald-green Jeep wasn't there. Instead, she followed J.J. over to his truck and climbed inside. Patrick climbed into the seat behind her and she watched as the rest of the group got into their vehicles and headed out of the lot.

J.J. was unusually silent on the ride, as was Patrick. When Jen again attempted asking what had happened to call them all in, J.J. just answered that Marc would explain when they got to her house. "I don't know all of the details right now so I don't have a lot to tell you."

As they passed Taco King, her favorite fast-food restaurant, Jen leaned towards the window and sniffed. Even though she knew it was just her imagination, she could swear she could smell the nachos. Her stomach rumbled in anticipation, as though she needed a reminder that she hadn't eaten in about ten hours. "I don't suppose we could stop for breakfast, could we?"

"Sorry, but no can do."

She sighed and slumped in her seat. "I know. But I don't remember if I have any food at the house and I haven't had breakfast yet."

"I'm sure we can take care of it later but for now, we're not stopping anywhere." Patrick reached forward from the back seat to put a re-assuring hand on her shoulder. "Tell you what, when we get back, I'll personally go get you some Crunchy-Os, okay?"

Jen burst into laughter at the reference to her favorite childhood cereal. "You're never go-ing to let me live that down, are you?"

"Nope," he sat back, and Jen knew without having to look that he was smirking. She could feel it in his voice as he explained to J.J. "You guys know she was busted for shoplifting as a kid, right?"

"Say what?" J.J. shot a questioning glance over at Jen.

"Yep. When we were younger, Jen refused to eat anything but Crunchy-Os. Mom got so fed up with it that she decided she wouldn't buy her any more Crunchy-Os, so Jen decided to take it into her own hands, literally. We got a call from the manager of the store down the road because he busted her trying to walk out the store with a box of Crunchy-Os."

"Come on," Jen protested. "I was maybe five."

She crossed her arms over her chest and pretended to pout while the men laughed at her expense. Thankfully, they managed to compose themselves again by the time they pulled up to her house. Jen and Patrick hopped out of the truck, followed quickly by J.J. Marc was already waiting on the sidewalk, as was Ty, and Mike pulled up and parked on the side of the road behind them. As they walked up to her front door, Jen asked, "Can you tell me what's going on yet?"

"Once we're inside, I promise." Marc answered.

With a sigh, Jen fished her keys out of her pocket and unlocked the front door. To her surprise, Marc stopped her as she tried to head inside, instead motioning for Ty and Mike to head in first. Only after they did a full sweep of the house and called out that it was clear did Marc let her enter.

Jen shot a look at the group, including Troy

and her brother, and stomped inside. "Okay, you seriously need to tell me what the hell is going on here. All this cloak and dagger crap is getting annoying."

"Someone tried to kill you in the hospital last night." Marc leaned on his crutches and leveled his gaze at her. "We take that kind of thing very seriously."

"Someone tried to kill me?" Jen blinked at him, wide eyed, before sinking down onto her couch. "Are you serious?" She looked around the rest of the group. "Of course you are. Who was it?" Then the real question, the one she probably should have asked first, finally occurred to her. "Why?"

"We haven't heard what the other guy is saying yet. Joel and his people caught him before he got to your room, but both he and Joel was taken into custody last night. I have contacts down at the station, so as soon as he starts talking, we'll know."

"Why was Joel arrested?"

"Joel's a hybrid, which is obviously related to a werewolf. When he stopped the assassin, he hurt the guy, apparently pretty badly. But because he's a hybrid, he was automatically taken in."

Hybrids were the offspring of a werewolf and a human. When the two join, their children are either full-blooded werewolves or half human and half werewolf, commonly referred to as a hybrid. All of the medical crew on staff during lunar events at North Bank hospital, at least in the lycanthrope wing, were hybrids. The main reason for this was that hybrids are automatically immune to lycanthropy so if they were attacked by a werewolf during a lunar event, they would not become infected.

Joel's father had been a werewolf and his mother a human, so he had inherited half of his mother's human genes and wasn't a full werewolf.

"What about Sahara and the kids? Are they okay?" Joel's wife, Sahara, was also Jen's best friend. Nicholas, the middle of their three kids, had inherited the hybrid gene, but Joel's older son Don and baby Collin had only received human genes. While full-blooded werewolves were incapable of producing human children, hybrids had a chance of "breeding out," or having full human children.

"They're fine. I think the kids are over at Sahara's parents' place and Sahara's at the police station trying to get Joel released."

"Couldn't they just get the video from the hospital? If there was an assassin there, that shows that Joel didn't do anything wrong." Jen looked around the group, holding Troy's eyes the longest. As Joel's best friend, she wasn't sure why he was here with her instead of kicking down walls trying to get his best friend released. Unlike her mild-mannered friend, Troy had an impressive temper, as Jen well knew. Knowing that Joel was incarcerated couldn't possibly be sitting well with him.

"She already has them." Patrick stepped closer and sat on the couch next to Jen. "Don't worry; Joel and Sahara are both going to be fine."

J.J. nodded in agreement. "For right now, our first priority was to get you somewhere safe because we weren't sure if the assassin was alone or working with someone else. Besides, anyone ballsy enough to break into a lunar wing on a full moon has to have a backup plan."

Jen nodded, remembering the commotion she had heard outside her cell the previous night. Only then did she realize that the disturbance had been directly related to her. She looked around the room, less at the people in it and more at the room itself. "Are we sure I'm safe here?"

Marc nodded. "Nobody else tried to get close to you last night and nobody tried to follow us here. Your address hasn't been on record since before you came to work with us, so there isn't any other way to track you here."

The team stayed with her for a few hours, partly to make her feel safer, and partly to make sure that they had been correct about nobody following her home. As her teammates packed up to leave, Jen called over to Sahara's house to see if they were home yet.

When Sahara answered the phone, Jen let out a sigh of relief. "You're home, good. Is Joel home too?"

"Yeah, he's in the shower getting the jail stink off him right now. Are you okay?"

"I'm good. Do you mind if I come over for a bit?"

"'Course not. Could you stop and pick up a bottle of syrup on your way?"

When Jen told the team that she was going to the Peters' house, Marc agreed. "You go do what you need to do. It looks like the danger's over for now, so we'll head out too."

Troy and Patrick insisted on going with her, whether it was for her protection or because Sahara always had a fully stocked fridge, Jen wasn't sure. Either way, she couldn't really argue because she would have to catch a ride with one of them; her truck was still over at Joel and Sahara's house where she had left it the previous evening. She, Patrick, and Troy all piled into Troy's old, beat-up car and headed out.

"When are you going to fix this old beater?" Patrick asked as he wedged himself into the backseat among piles of equipment. Troy stored most of his belongings in the trunk, but items he used regularly lived in the backseat for easy access.

"It's not a beater," Troy responded, pretending to be offended. "This car is a classic. I've been working on it when I have time for the last couple years, it's just taking a bit longer than I expected."

"What have you fixed so far? It still smells like ancient gym socks back here."

"Haven't gotten to the interior yet, all the work I've been doing was under the hood." He revved the engine in demonstration of his handiwork. "I'll get to that eventually."

"Might want to consider doing it sooner rather than later, or just not having other people in your car until then. Seriously!" Patrick lifted half a cheeseburger by its greasy wrapper. "This is disgusting!"

"Might be pretty bad now," Troy agreed, "but it'll be amazing by the time I'm finished with it."

"You had a lot of model cars when you were a child, didn't you?" Jen asked.

Troy sent a sideways glance her direction, confused by the change in topic. "Yeah, why?"

She nodded sagely. "I've noticed a trend in people who had a lot of models while they were growing up. When they get older, they become deluded into believing that, given enough paint, anything would look good." Patrick howled in amusement at her statement, but Troy didn't look nearly as amused.

# Chapter 2

Don, Sahara and Joel's eight-year-old son, opened the door for them when they arrived, breaking into a grin when he saw who was there. "Aunt Jen! I didn't know you were coming over today," he opened the door wider when he spotted the rest of the group. "Hi, Troy," he said as they stepped inside, but he quieted and eyed the last one suspiciously. "Who're you?"

"This is Patrick, he's my big brother," Jen introduced as she handed a couple pieces of sour lemon candy down to the boy. "There's one for each of you, I expect you to share." It had been a number of years since Patrick had seen the children, so it was no surprise that Don didn't recognize him.

Don's face spread into another smile, even

wider than before. "Cool, thanks." He imme-diately stuck one piece into his mouth and headed off to distribute the others.

"You'd better not be giving them candy," Sahara's voice called out from the kitchen. "The last thing I need today is dealing with them on a sugar buzz." As Sahara walked out of the kitchen, Jen noticed that she looked a lot more tired than she had in a long while. There were dark circles under her eyes and her eyes them-selves looked slightly bloodshot. She looked over at the group. "Well, it looks like you made it out okay."

Even Sahara's hair seemed to have faded from the vibrant rainbow of colors that it had previously been. While it was still multicol-ored, the colors appeared duller. Her eyes must have been sore from a night without enough sleep because instead of wearing her contact lenses as she usually did, she had her old wire-framed glasses on. As usual, she was dressed in a brightly colored short-sleeved shirt and ratty jeans, without shoes. To look at her, one would never guess that she was the mastermind behind one of the most successful herbal shops in the state.

Jen walked across the room to hug her friend. "I'm sorry, Sahara, I had no idea that something like that was going to happen."

"Of course you didn't, how could you have?" Sahara smiled up at her. "And Joel should be out of the shower by now. He's going to want to see for himself that you're okay, too."

As she finished speaking, a tall man with hair almost as black as Jen's came out of one of the back rooms. He was dressed in a pair of jeans that had both knees ripped out and a brown leather belt that looked like it had seen better years, let alone days. His chest was covered in tattoos: one of a wolf, another of a partially full moon, and yet another of an enormous wolf standing guard in front of a woman and three small children.

"Did you get your pancakes?" Joel asked as she saw Jen and her group. When he had helped her check into the hospital the night before, he had promised to bring Jen a plate of pancakes if she didn't turn into a werewolf. Now understanding what had happened, Jen understood why the pancakes had not been forthcoming.

She shook her head. "Nobody came in at all until Marc unlocked the door in the morning. I see you added to your guardian tattoo." The last time Jen had seen Joel's tattoos, the large wolf had only been standing over two children. The third one looked brighter and fresher, so she guessed he had gotten it updated fairly recently.

"Yeah. Collin's turning one here pretty soon, so I figured I'd better hurry up and get it fixed." He walked over and hugged Jen as well. "I'm just glad you're okay. I was worried." He let go and stepped back. "I can't believe nobody brought you your pancakes; I was bringing them when that asshole showed up."

He walked over to have a seat on the couch. "I'm just glad I was able to stop him before he got to you."

"What happened? All that the guys told me was that someone came after me and you stopped him."

Joel nodded. "A couple of us had our eyes

on him before he made a move. He came in saying he was there to make sure that a friend of his had made it to check in and kept asking if he could go down the hall to make sure his friend was okay because it was her first lunar event. We wouldn't let him, so he kept hanging around, watching all of us.

"One of the guys had already contacted security because we aren't supposed to have any humans in the wing, especially after the moon comes up, so they were going to have him escorted out. He must have realized he was about to get tossed out because he made a run for the gate to the undetermined wing." The undetermined wing had been where Jen spent the night, where the guards watched people who weren't sure whether or not they had been infected with lycanthropy.

"Like I said, I was bringing you your pancakes, so I was right there when all the shouting started. The guy pulls a gun out of his pocket, looked like it was homemade, and tries to duck around me." He accepted the cup of tea that Sahara offered him and took a sip before continuing. "So, I grab him as he's trying to go around and the gun goes off. Barely missed me, I have no idea where the bullet went." He took another sip of tea. "I didn't want to wait and find out how many rounds he was packing, so I grabbed him by an arm and dropped him to the ground.

"That's actually why I got brought in; apparently, I broke his arm while I was taking him down and he probably had a pretty bad concussion from slamming his head into the floor, it is concrete, after all. But that's about when the security guys got there. They took his gun and carried him out. I think they took him off to get his arm set and have a look at his head before handing him over to the cops." He took another drink once he was finished speaking.

"How did you know he was after me?" Jen was curious.

"Because you were the friend he was asking after. Aside from not allowing humans into the lunar wing, that was what really got my suspicions up. That's the main reason we really started to keep an eye on him and why nobody would tell him anything. I figured, by how quiet you'd been about the whole thing, the chances of you having told someone that I've never even met about it were pretty slim."

Jen nodded. "But you're okay now, right? They aren't pressing charges against you or anything, are they?"

"Nah. Once Sahara got there with the security footage, there wasn't much left for them to say." He eyed Jen suspiciously. "You aren't going to go out and do anything stupid, are you?"

"No, I'm just going to go talk to the guy, if I can get close enough. I think I at least deserve to know who's trying to kill me."

"In that case, wait a couple minutes. I need to get dressed but I'm coming with you." He held up a hand when she started to argue. "First, I need to let my supervisor know that I've been released. Second, my van's still there, so I need to go pick it up anyway. Third, if you think I'm going to let you go back there without me, you're crazy. Someone tried to kill you on my watch, and I take that very personally." He stood up and headed for the bedroom. "And on the way back, we can stop and I'll buy you some pancakes."

Jen looked over at Troy. "Since Joel's coming with me, why don't you stay here and give Sahara a hand with the kids? She looks exhausted."

Troy nodded, understanding that what Jen was really requesting was for him to be there to keep Sahara and the kids safe, just in case. Even though the would-be assassin was in custody, there had been far too much violence in town lately. She wasn't willing to take any more chances than she had to with her best friends and their family.

Once Joel was dressed, he followed Jen and Patrick out to Jen's Jeep, which was still parked at the curb where she had left it when Joel took her to the hospital the previous night. Just to be sure, Jen walked around it, checking to make sure that there weren't any obvious signs of tampering. "Call me paranoid if you want to," she said to the men as she walked, "but I think I have reason to be suspicious."

There was no argument so once Jen was satisfied, she let everyone climb in. They headed down to the hospital and parked in the volunteer section, next to Joel's van. Joel led the way inside and headed directly for his supervisor's office.

Before they got there, however, they were stopped by hospital security. Only a couple steps inside the door, a large man in a blue uniform and reflective sunglasses stopped them. "I'm sorry, but nobody is allowed in right now. The hospital's on lockdown."

"What's going on?" Joel asked.

"There was a prisoner in for medical treatment that escaped. He's considered dangerous, so the hospital is being searched. Nobody goes in or out until that's finished."

A sinking feeling appeared in Jen's stomach. "The man that got caught in the lunar wing last night? Is he the one that escaped?"

The security officer nodded. "There's no reason to worry, the fugitive isn't a werewolf. He was just caught trying to kill one." He looked from Jen to Joel, and then over to Patrick. "He was probably just a nut from one of those extremist groups, trying to get Weres exterminated."

"Yeah, well, the person he was trying to

exterminate was me so I wanted to find out why he wanted me dead." Jen had no clue what he meant by extremist groups; maybe she should take Sahara's advice and start watching the news occasionally after all.

The officer reached up and lowered his shades so that he could see over them more clearly. "You're a Were?"

Jen shook her head. "I got scratched by one, so I was in here just in case I had been infected. I didn't shift, so no, I'm not a Were." She glared up at the officer, disregarding the fact that he was a good four inches taller and probably had a hundred pounds on her. "Would it matter if I was? The last time I checked, being a Were wasn't illegal."

"Nope, nothing wrong with that. But if you are the person he was after, then I think my boss might have a few questions for you." He looked around behind him at the handful of security officers that were still further inside. He waved over at one that seemed to be directing traffic between the security and other hospital personnel.

"Take her to see Richards," he instructed the

man when he arrived. "Let him know that she was the target last night, so I'm pretty sure he's going to want to talk with her."

The younger man nodded and escorted them inside. "All three, or just the one?" he called back.

"Go ahead and take all three. Just make sure they all stay together."

The younger officer nodded and led them further into the hospital. He brought them into a different section of the hospital, where the administration offices were located. There, he led them into an office and closed the door behind them.

A pair of men was arguing in the office, one in a security uniform and the other in a police officer's uniform. As the door clicked closed, both men looked up to see who had intruded on the argument. "What do you want, Justin?" The man dressed in security gear asked. "Aren't you supposed to be helping to search the hospital?"

"Steve told me to bring these people to you. The lady was the target that the fugitive was after last night. He figured you'd want to meet with her."

The security supervisor rose from his seat and walked around the desk, stepped closer to Jen, and stuck out a hand. "Sam Richards. Have a seat." He indicated a couple of chairs that were set against a wall. "And who are these?" he asked as he looked at Patrick and Joel.

"I'm a volunteer in the lunar wing," Joel explained. "I was the one taken to jail last night when he went after her."

Sam nodded and looked over at Patrick. "And you are?"

"He's my brother," Jen answered before he could reply, "and he's staying with me. The guard at the door said you lost the guy, is that right?"

"Now, hang on a minute, that's not what happened."

"Jen?" The police officer stepped around Sam to have a look at her. "Why am I not surprised to see you wrapped up in this?"

"You know her?" Sam asked the officer.

"Of course I know her. She spent most of

last month making herself a right pain in the ass at the station."

"Officer Jenkins?" Jen asked as he approached. "Ah, hell." She held both hands up. "I swear, I didn't do anything this time." For most of the previous month, Jen had spent a lot of time at the local police station, sometimes to file complaints against members of Hyatt Response, a rival response company that had been harassing her, and sometimes she had been at the police station waiting for someone to pick her up after having been arrested in altercations with the same response company. Since the altercations had stopped and the harassment and mutual assault cases had stopped, all of the charges against Jen had been dropped, thanks in no small part due to the officer now standing before her.

"Well, obviously somebody did something. After all, isn't that why we're here?" Sam interrupted. He looked down at Jen. "So, if you really were the target last night, do you know why he was after you?"

"Could be any number of different reasons,"

she shrugged. "It all just depends on who it was that was trying to kill me."

Sam blinked at her admission. "Do you really have that many people who want you dead?"

She shrugged again. "Less now than I had a couple weeks ago, but yeah, I guess there's still some out there. That's actually why I'm here; I wanted to see who it was that tried last night, maybe even find out why he was after me." She looked up at Sam. "But I guess that's not going to happen, now is it?"

Officer Jenkins snickered and picked up a photograph from the desk. He handed it over to her, over Sam's protests. "Do you know who he is?"

"You can't just hand evidence over like that," Sam objected.

"She's not a suspect," Jenkins responded. "If she can help identify the assailant, that makes all of our jobs easier."

Jen accepted the picture and examined it. It was obviously a still from the hospital's security videos and showed a section of the entrance to the lunar wing. There were a handful of people in the photo and Jen wasn't immediately sure of which person had been the attacker. "The only person in here I recognize is Joel and one of the security officers that we walked past last night while I was checking in."

Joel leaned over and pointed to a man that was standing a few feet away from the doors leading into the secure area of the lunar wing. "That's him."

Jen looked more closely at the man he had indicated, but he was a very small person in a very large and equally crowded area. "Do you have a larger picture of him?"

Jenkins dug through more photos on the desk and handed her another. This one was an enlargement of the previous photo but now Jen was at least able to make out some of the man's characteristics.

He was heavyset, with light brown hair that was mostly tucked under a baseball cap. He wore a denim jacket and blue jeans, nothing surprising there. However, he had what appeared to be a scar that ran down along his right eyebrow, dividing it in half. She pointed at the scar as she looked up at Joel. "Is this a scar, or a glitch in the picture?"

Joel leaned over to get a better look. "I think that's a scar. Do you know him?"

She had expected to recognize the assassin, for him to be the same man who had been trying to kill her for the last couple weeks. One glance at the blown-up image confirmed that it was not the same man.

Jen shook her head. "He looks kind of familiar from somewhere, but I can't place him."

Sam tried to take the picture back but Jen wouldn't let him. "I want to take this back to the office and give it to my boss. That way, the other people I work with can keep an eye out for him too. You never know, one of them might recognize him." She tucked it into one of the pockets on the side of her leg. "Besides, if that guy's after me, I want to show it to my neighbors and stuff. I'd like to know as early as possible if he's coming anywhere near my house, my family, or my friends."

He tried to protest, but Jenkins stopped him. "You can get another picture but letting her have that one is about the easiest move you can make right now."

"What's that supposed to mean?"

"Did you hear about the entire Hyatt crew getting hospitalized about a week ago?" Jenkins asked. When Sam nodded, he continued. "That was her, you know."

"Her?" Sam looked down at Jen doubtfully. "You're telling me that she's capable of taking on a strike team?"

As Jen's eyes narrowed, Jenkins stepped between her and Sam. "She's on a strike team, too, you know, so I wouldn't underestimate her."

"Response team," Jen interrupted to correct him. She never had understood why so many people referred to response teams as strike teams as though they were the same thing. Response teams like hers were sent out at the beginning of any problem involving the paranormal, tasked with diffusing the situation as best they could. Rarely was violence involved. Strike teams, on the other hand, were deployed when response teams failed or if the paranormal target proved to be too dangerous to leave alone. They used lethal weaponry almost exclusively and their charge was not to calm the target, it was to destroy.

"If you don't have the guy here, and apparently you don't even know who he was, then maybe I should just leave." She stood up and headed for the door. "That was my only reason for being here, so if you don't have anything else, I have things I need to do."

"Hang on a second, you can't just walk out like that." Sam stepped between her and the door.

"Why not?"

"We still have some questions for you." He gestured back to her seat. His eyes, while initially welcoming, had hardened into suspicion.

"Like what?" She wasn't about to go sit down until she found out what he wanted.

"You said that there were a lot of people that wanted you dead. Care to fill us in on that?" He pulled a small notebook from his shirt pocket and a pen.

"Would if I could, but I'm not sure I know who all of them are."

"What's that supposed to mean?" Sam looked up from his notes.

Jen thought, but only for a moment. "Well, there was the psychic who's been trying to kill me for a while now. Haven't seen him for a few days but I'm not sure he was ever located." She looked over at Jenkins. "Was he?"

Jenkins shook his head. "Nope. By the time we got there, he was long gone and there haven't been any reports of him anywhere since."

"Is this the psychic that you're talking about?" Sam asked.

"Nope. Thought it would be at first, but it's a different guy. Let's see," Jen thought for a moment. "There's the Hyatt guys, but we've already covered them. He's not any of them either. Then there's the Were that attacked me. I think he's been put down but he was already reported to have been put down once before I met him, so that doesn't mean much." She looked over at Joel and Patrick. "Who am I forgetting?"

"Well, there's anyone else that the demon thing might have taken control of, that's always a possibility."

The demon Patrick referred to was a hideous demon that had been inhabiting the body of a dreamwalker who had made contact with Jen. In fact, it had been the contact from the dreamwalker that had allowed Jen to close the portal to Derathim, a place that most people knew as hell, that had allowed the demon to possess him in the first place. Although Jen only knew of one person who had been possessed by the demon, that didn't mean that he had been the only one.

"True. Just because he's gone, that doesn't mean that he doesn't still have some sort of hold on people here." She thought for another moment before continuing. "My high school English teacher, she swore that if she had to read another of my awful essays, she'd personally put me out of her misery.

"Ty, my teammate, he wants me dead because he thinks I was trying to kill him a while ago." She looked up at Sam and quickly explained. "I wasn't, really, but he hadn't ever ridden with me before, so it's understandable."

She thought again. "I know there's a couple of cops on the force that wouldn't mind seeing me in the morgue and I'm pretty sure that whoever was driving the bus that stops in front of the hospital was trying to take me out while I was turning into the driveway.

"Do you really want me to keep going? I can probably come up with more, if you really want me to."

"No, I think that'll be everything." Sam had long since stopped taking notes on Jen's list of would-be assassins, a look of weary resignation on his face.

"So can I go now?" When he just waved a hand at her in response, she walked out the door, followed by Joel and Patrick, who were both trying their best not to fall over laughing.

# Chapter 3

When Jen crawled out of bed the next morning, she discovered that the living room was a lot less crowded than it should have been. Troy Franklin, her part-time bodyguard and roommate, was busily snoring the morning away in his recliner as usual, but the couch looked barren and lonely without Patrick lying on top of it. She looked slowly around the room, wondering if perhaps he had fallen asleep somewhere else but he was nowhere to be seen. His blanket was folded on the arm of the couch and his suitcase still leaned against the wall, so she knew that he hadn't gone far.

Cautiously, she stepped towards the dark kitchen, wondering if he had experienced a restless night and was simply sitting up and watching the sunrise as he used to do when they were younger. If that was the case, she mused to herself hopefully, he might have already started the coffee pot.

Disappointingly, neither Patrick nor a ready pot of coffee awaited her in the kitchen. After looking around, she started a pot herself and set out to check the rest of the house while it brewed. Since her house was small, it didn't take too long to verify that her brother was nowhere within it. With a sigh, she headed into her bedroom to get dressed.

If Patrick was out doing something stupid, she would have to go find him, and she wasn't going to do it in her pajamas.

As she walked out of her room, she was greeted by the aromatic welcome of fresh coffee. She headed down the hall, telling herself that she really needed to start remembering to set the timer on the pot when she went to bed at night because there was no better way to wake up than with coffee ready.

She jumped when she walked into the kitchen and discovered Patrick there, pouring the coffee into a pair of cups. He smirked at her reaction and handed her one of them. "Well, good morning to you too."

"Where the hell were you?" she asked as she took the cup. "I was looking everywhere for you."

"Sorry about that. Some more of my crew got into town last night, so I took them out to breakfast and showed them the site we'd be working at." Patrick was a site supervisor for a rather large construction company. His company had taken a contract in town, so Patrick had arrived early to visit with Jen before the project started. He took a drink of his coffee. "You were still asleep, so I didn't want to bother you about it."

Jen nodded and took a sip of her beverage. "I had forgotten about all that, considering what's been going on. I just woke up, and you weren't here, so I thought something must have happened to you."

Patrick sighed. "Come on, you should know better than that. If something bad was happening, I would let you know."

"When is your project supposed to open?"

"Pretty soon. I have a few more meetings

scheduled and a few of my men haven't arrived yet but I think I have most of the preliminary work taken care of so we can get started as soon as everyone's here. Maybe another week, at the latest."

"Hey, what's all the noise about?" Troy yawned as he stumbled into the kitchen. "Why's everyone up so early, did something happen?" Troy was a hybrid, part human and part were-wolf, and looked every bit the part, particularly first thing in the morning. His scruffy beard, which Jen was sure contained every shade of brown in the Crayola box, stuck out from his face in every direction possible. As he scanned the room through half-lidded eyes, he absently reached one hand to smooth the facial hair back into place.

"No, everything's okay," Patrick answered. He poured another cup and handed it over be-fore picking up his bag of tools from the table and walking out of the room.

After his first sip, Troy sniffed a couple times. "Spray paint?" He raised an eyebrow at Jen and walked out towards the living room after Patrick. "Hey! What are you doing to my chair?"

Jen rushed out after him, but stopped about halfway into the living room. She had to blink a few times to confirm what she was seeing wasn't part of some weird dream. Patrick was kneeling on the floor next to Troy's recliner with a stencil in one hand and a can of black spray paint in the other. Even at the angle she was at, Jen could see the smirk on her brother's face.

A few seconds later, Patrick stepped back to observe his handiwork. On the side of the chair, in fairly straight letters, was the term "Bark-O-Lounger".

Even as Jen tried not to laugh too loudly, she could tell that Troy wasn't truly offended. He and Patrick had enjoyed a tumultuous relationship since Patrick had arrived in town and discovered that Jen had a strange man sleeping on her couch.

Not that Jen blamed him, of course. Pretty much anyone would be suspicious, given the circumstances. However, their feud had quickly settled into petty acts of minor sabotage, which Jen found entertaining enough to not bother putting a stop to.

"There. You insisted on bringing that flea-ridden chair into the house, the least we can do is warn other people so they know it's yours."

Jen couldn't hold it in any longer. She slumped onto the couch, set her coffee onto the floor next to her, and started wiping tears from her eyes as she collapsed into laughter.

Her laughter only grew worse with Troy's only objection. "I don't have fleas, thank you." He didn't seem to notice that he was absently scratching the hair of his beard even as he spoke.

Once she calmed down, Jen decided it was time to turn on the news. It wasn't generally her favorite show to watch, most of the time she preferred cartoons, but she was curious as to whether there had been any more information released about her would-be assassin. She clicked through channels, trying to remember where the news could be found, until she gave up and handed the remote over to Troy. "I need the news," she explained.

"Since when do you watch the news?"

"Since now," she sighed. "Apparently there is more going on out in the world than I thought."

"Looking for anything particular?"

"I have no idea. I know there's some sort of anti-werewolf group or something that's been causing problems, so I should probably know something about that. And I want to see if there's anything on the guy from the hospital." She thought a moment longer. "And there's something Lewis said a while ago about energy from Derathim causing problems for the whole paranormal community. I should keep an eye on that stuff too." Lewis was a ghost who wandered from area to area across town, often stopping to hang out with Sahara and Jen while he was in the neighborhood. He had proven to be a rich source of information about activities throughout the paranormal community and was the only reason she knew of the energy issue to begin with.

As Troy flipped through the channels, Patrick picked up his tools and stuffed them back into his bag to take out to his truck. The odor of fresh paint still clung to everything but it was too cold and wet outside to leave the doors open so the house could air out. Instead, Jen just stuck her nose in her coffee cup to mask the scent, tucked her feet up beneath her on the couch, and watched the news.

"Is it just me, or are there a lot more commercials lately than there used to be?" she asked to nobody in particular.

"Yeah, I think there are, too. Give it a few more years, and your hour-long show will only have twenty minutes of actual show in it, the rest will just be advertisements." Troy answered as he flopped in his chair.

They suffered through a bit from the local animal shelter, which explained about how many pets had been abandoned over the last year and how the shelter couldn't keep up with demand. Jen felt sorry for all the animals that were kept cooped up in there but she knew that she didn't have time for a pet and wouldn't be doing any of the animals a favor by adopting one. However, since she did feel bad about the situation, she made a mental note to make a donation towards expanding the building and helping to take care of the animals that were already there.

There was a quick story about an explosion in a gas line below a nearby town. That story caused Jen to pay a little more attention because that was the town that she, Troy, Patrick, and the rest of her team had been in just a few days ago. As she thought about it, she realized that the explosion they were talking about hadn't been caused by a gas leak at all but instead had been caused by one of Troy's incendiaries. She and her group had had good reason for blowing up a small portion of the underground area there, after all, that was where they had battled the demon that had inhabited the dreamwalker but she still felt bad about the small collapse that they had caused. Apparently, there had been some structural damage to a few of the businesses above the explosion.

There was a report of a break-in at a local jewelry store that caught her attention as well. The reporter stood outside the business that had been robbed, explaining that the theft was the largest that this particular jeweler had experienced. Over five million dollars' worth of jewelry had vanished in the middle of the night and the thief had managed to get in, get the goods, and get out without tripping the store's alarm system. When the store manager arrived in the morning, he had discovered that most of the jewelry in their vault was missing.

She let out a low whistle at the dollar amount that had been stolen, a reaction that was cut short as the report cut to a clip of the store manager, explaining what he believed had happened. "It had to have been a mage, or a psychic. There's no way a normal person would have been able to get away with this without anyone being alerted."

Jen narrowed her eyes at the shopkeeper's assertion that it couldn't have been a 'normal' person, as though mages weren't normal. For years, she had seen the same kind of comments directed toward Todd, her twin brother, who happened to be a mage. She couldn't count the number of times she had heard that at least she was normal for not having magic. As though there was something weird with her brother. She could feel the heat rising up the back of her neck as she thought more about it and made a mental note to call Todd later to check in on him.

"Sounds more like an inside job, to me," Patrick commented as he walked back into the room. "Places like that have hellacious security, so unless you have a master override code and a handful of keys that go with it, the alarms are going to go off." He dropped onto the couch next to Jen. "Especially if they're saying the vault was broken into. Vaults in those places are handprint scan locked. Without the right hand, they don't open."

Jen nodded. "I was just thinking that maybe someone realized they had forgotten their anniversary and needed something, fast," she snickered. Not that she needed to bother, of course. Patrick knew full well about her response to mages being unfairly singled out all the time. Todd was his brother as well, of course, so he shared many of her views on the matter.

Finally, the last story was about the hospital escape, although there wasn't much more information than what Jen already knew. A picture of the would-be assassin was displayed on the screen and viewers were encouraged to keep an eye out for him. He had still not been identified but the reporter warned everyone that he was considered armed and extremely dangerous. "If you see this man, do not approach him. Call the police immediately and get out of the area." The image they showed was the same one that Jen had been given, which still rested where she had dropped it on the kitchen counter the previous day.

"I guess that means he wasn't at the hospital," Troy commented. "Great." He looked over at Jen. "You okay?"

"Yeah, I'm fine," she nodded. "He's probably off hiding somewhere and he'll turn up pretty soon." Despite the bravado, she was more concerned than she let on. She didn't like the idea of having someone try to kill her and she liked the idea of him getting away even less. Having his image splashed all over the news gave her a little comfort, the viewing audience was guaranteed to be larger than just those she could personally show the picture to, so the chances were much higher of his being caught now that the story had been aired.

Once the news was over, an obnoxious sit-com came on and Jen threw the remote back to Troy. "I'm going to go check the mail. You can watch whatever you want." She climbed to her feet and headed for the door. "Don't worry," she called over her shoulder, "I'm only going out the curb, so I don't need backup." She ducked out the door and closed it behind her as Troy threw a magazine at her.

The mailbox, neglected for the last few days, was stuffed with bills, mailers, and other assorted junk. In the middle of the stack were the latest editions of her video game and handgun magazines. The video game subscription she had maintained since high school but the handgun one was new. She had only started that one since starting at New World Response. The pistol they had issued her worked just fine for what she needed but she knew that she would need to upgrade soon. If she was going to do that, she needed to know what was out on the market.

As she walked back in the door, her phone started ringing. She dropped the stack of mail onto the couch and answered the phone.

"Hey, were you still coming over today?" Even over the phone, Sahara sounded tired, and Jen wondered how much sleep her friend had been getting lately.

"Of course," she answered automatically. "What was I coming over for?" Jen vaguely remembered having agreed to be at Sahara's house that afternoon, but she couldn't remember why.

"We're making the Soul tokens today, remember? It's only a few days until the Festival."

Long ago, the Festival of Souls had started out as a day of honoring the dead and making peace with the restless spirits that still walked among the living. People started to set out tokens to the spirits, to appease them for the upcoming year. Many of these tokens consisted of small pieces of bread, slices of fruit, small bowls of beer, wine, or other liquors, scraps of cloth, ribbon, and other colorful fabrics but different tokens were left out for the recently deceased. Those were of the more expensive variety, including coins, perfumes, and small pieces of jewelry.

As years passed, however, the tradition

changed to one of excitement and joy, where people not only paid homage to those who had passed but also celebrated the life that remained. The Festival was marked by parades, with people dressed in fancy clothes and bright costumes. Music and noisemakers could be heard everywhere because the loud sounds were supposed to keep any angry spirits at bay for the night. Now, however, drunken revelers were far more common than vengeful ghosts.

Ever the traditionalist, Sahara still made tokens, small fetishes that she hung in the trees outside her house. These tokens were stuffed with herbal mixtures that Sahara whipped up at her shop, feathers that she had gathered throughout the year, and sometimes even pebbles that she, Joel, and the boys picked up on their annual vacations to the beach.

"Right, I knew that." Jen mentally kicked herself. With everything that had been happening, she had completely forgotten about the festival. "I'll be there in just a few, okay?"

"Okay, I'll see you then."

As Jen hung up the phone, she looked over at the guys. "I'm supposed to be at Sahara's, helping out with the Soul tokens. You guys coming, or are you going to stay here and watch TV?"

Troy turned the television off, stepped into his boots, and proclaimed he was ready to go. Patrick, on the other hand, looked at his watch. "I have another meeting in forty-five minutes, so I can go with you but I'll have to leave pretty quickly."

"No problem," Jen responded. "You stay here. Go to your meeting and we'll catch back up with you later. We'll be fine."

"You sure? Because I can come for a little bit."

"No, its fine." She hugged her brother. "We'll see you later. Have fun at your meeting." She and Troy headed out the door, leaving Patrick to lock up.

"I know we're headed to Sahara's place. But what are we supposed to be doing there?" Troy asked as they climbed into the Jeep.

"We're going to help Sahara and the kids make the Soul tokens." She glanced at him as she swung onto the street. "Have you ever made them before?"

He shook his head. "Not since I was a kid."

He buckled his seat belt and pulled it tight against him. "I didn't know people still made those; most people I know just buy them."

"I know, but this is Sahara. She likes doing things like that the old-fashioned way. Besides, I have to agree with her on one point: how is buying a pre-made token going to appease the spirits? That's the whole idea, after all and I can't see the spirits being too pleased about having a bunch of pre-fabricated, store-bought stuff left out for them."

When Jen and Troy pulled up in front of Sahara's house, they could tell that the token-making was already well under way. Small scented pouches hung from the trees and bushes outside the front door and small grains were scattered across the sidewalk. On the doorstep, a small bucket and scoop sat, silently waiting for more of the grains contained within to be scattered in tribute.

Jen walked in with barely a knock, not that it mattered because there was noise everywhere inside. The radio was turned up and music filled the house. Sahara and her three children, Don, Nicholas, and Collin, were gathered around the kitchen table with bowls, boxes, jars, and bags of material scattered everywhere. Nicholas's face lit up when he saw the arrivals. "You made it!"

"Yep, of course I made it. You know I wouldn't miss this for the world," Jen answered as she ruffled his hair. "What do we have here?"

Nicholas held up the pouch that he was busily stuffing. "I got ribbon and pinecones in here. Me and Don went out and picked up all the pinecones this morning." He pointed to a bowl of small pinecones, still sticky with sap.

"Awesome!" Jen sat down in between Nicholas and Don. Sahara was busily showing Collin how to put his small pile of goods into a pouch but Collin seemed much more interested in trying to eat the materials than putting them into the sachet.

"Mom made us new costumes this year, too!" Don piped in. "Want to see them?"

"Once we're done with this, then yeah, I want to see them." Although Sahara preferred the older traditions, the kids loved to dress up in bright costumes like everyone else. They were kids, after all, and Sahara always indulged them. Secretly, Jen believed that Sahara actually liked the costumes every bit as much as the boys did, considering how much time she spent designing their garb.

They spent the next couple of hours making more tokens and setting them aside to be hung. Some would be placed outside with the ones Jen had already seen, others brought down to Sugar and Spice, Sahara's herbal shop. Still more would be placed in the boys' bedrooms, protective charms against malevolent spirits. "You need to make some for your house, too," Sahara explained to Jen as they worked. "With all the things that have been going on with you lately, I think you need them more than any of the rest of us do."

Jen tried to protest, but Sahara would hear none of it. She shoved a small mountain of supplies and a handful of pouches towards her. "Go on, make as many as you want." She looked at her friend thoughtfully for a moment before adding, "perhaps making some for your truck and your office would be a good idea, too."

With a sigh, knowing she had no other choice, Jen relented. She opened a pouch and stuffed it with a couple of feathers, some beach stones, and a snippet of grass from outside. "Okay, I made one. Happy now?"

"Nope. I won't be happy until you've made at least five." Sahara stood next to Jen, looking down at her with her hands on her hips. "And you're going to place these around your house, inside and out, and I think you should make one to carry with you, too."

"Come on, seriously?" Jen argued. "You don't really believe that these are going to keep me safe, do you?"

"Maybe, maybe not. But I, for one, would be a lot more comfortable discovering that you had them and didn't need them than if you needed them and didn't have them." Her face turned stern. "Besides, you know as well as I do that there is a lot of energy flow during the Festival, both light and dark. The least you can do is humor me on this."

Jen grudgingly worked on her tokens, until the front door burst open. Both she and Troy jumped to their feet, immediately ready to face the threat. A young woman with a long braid hanging down her back stumbled into the house. "Make it stop!" she moaned as she fell over on the couch, pulled the throw blanked over her head, and whimpered.

"Angie?" Jen dropped her project to rush to her friend's side. "What happened?"

"It's Eric, that's what happened." Eric was a poltergeist that haunted the house Angie lived in. She hadn't known about Eric when she bought the house and the two of them had only barely settled into an understanding. Nevertheless, Eric had continued to be a thorn in Angie's backside, inciting as much frustration in her as he possibly could.

"What did he do this time?" Sahara asked as she pulled the covers off Angie and offered her a cup of coffee. "And are you all right?"

Angie accepted the cup gratefully. "He started howling during the last full moon. He was up all night, just baying away at it." She looked at the assembled group. "It wasn't even like I could throw something at him to shut him up, everything just passes through him." She took another sip and continued. "I figured that it was just the one night, and I could handle that. But the next night, he's at it again! Not quite as loudly, but still howling away. Stupid poltergeist thinks he's a werewolf or something!"

Sahara did her best to soothe the poor girl, waving Jen back to her project before she fully burst out laughing. Given how disruptive Eric had been in the past, it was easy to imagine how much of a pest he could be now.

# Chapter 4

The next afternoon, Jen was called into the office for a meeting. She headed out to the office, wondering what she had done to get in trouble this time. Jen was well aware that she had a rough history and was known for getting herself into all sorts of trouble, sometimes without even knowing about it. As she drove, she ran back through the last few days, trying to see if she had stepped out of bounds somewhere, but she was at a loss.

When she got there, she discovered that the entire team had been called in, a welcome relief. Unless the whole team had screwed up, a possibility that she doubted, she wasn't in trouble after all. David Melrose, the team supervisor and head honcho of the company, was waiting for all of them in the basement situation room.

"As we all know," he raised his hands for the group to settle down and listen, "tomorrow is the Festival of Souls. Even though it's celebrated like a holiday, I want you all to remember that the Festival started out as a very powerful day. Spirits can still get pissed off just as easily as everybody else but tomorrow they'll all have a lot more power to do something about it.

"Also, I want to remind you that there are a lot of untrained mages and psychics out there and even more than that who just haven't been trained enough. Every year, it never fails; one of them will try to do something that's outside their power level, thinking that they can use the extra energy of the holiday to boost their own power level. While most of the time it's just the idiot that had the bright idea in the first place that gets hurt, there have been many times in the past that other people have gotten hurt, too.

"I want you all here and ready to go first thing in the morning tomorrow. The energy levels should start increasing at about eleven in the morning and should reach their peak at about five in the afternoon before they taper off again. Until the power levels are back to normal, consider yourselves on the clock." He looked around at the assembled group. "Any questions?"

Nobody answered, so he waved them away. "Go home, get some sleep. Tomorrow's going to be a big day."

Jen followed the rest of the group up the stairs and out of the office. "Guess there won't be any parade for us," she quipped.

"Nope," J.J. answered. "And so much for my plan of going home and getting sloshed to celebrate, too."

They each headed off their separate directions. As usual, Troy was waiting at Jen's truck when she got to it. "You can come in the building while I'm in there, you know."

"I know, but it's more comfortable out here." He dropped into the passenger seat. "C'mon, spill it. What was the big news?"

"We're all on duty tomorrow," she answered as she backed out onto the street. Horns sounded as she shifted into gear but she ignored them, as usual. "First thing in the morning until the power levels fall back to where they're supposed to be." She turned onto the highway, barely checking her mirrors as she went. "Probably until about midnight or so."

"But that means you're going to miss out on all the fun," he protested. "And so am I! You can't do this to me!"

"Suck it up, princess," she smirked at him. "You're more than welcome to go out on your own; nobody ever said you had to come with me."

"Hey, I'm here to protect you, not to go out partying while you're out in danger. Besides, I was just kidding."

"I know, and I know you had wanted to go out for a bit tomorrow, too. I'm just letting you know you can." She glanced over at him as she whipped past another car that was travelling far too slowly for her taste. "It's not like I'm going to be out there on my own, I'll have the rest of the team there with me."

They bickered about it for the rest of the drive home. As she pulled onto her street, Jen noticed that Patrick's truck was parked in its usual spot but now there was another beat-up pickup parked behind it, also emblazoned with his company's logo. As she parked, she noticed that there was something strange about the second truck, and had to walk over to investigate.

There were small Soul tokens hanging from every conceivable mounting point in and on the truck. A token hung every few inches along the rack that was mounted in the bed and a few even dangled from the tow hitch and the rear bumper. Inside the cab, there were tokens hanging from the rearview mirror, the garment hooks over the back windows, and off both sun visors. Even the front bumper proudly displayed a few of the charms.

Jen stared at the perplexing sight in a combination of shock and disbelief, but Troy was much more to the point. He burst out laughing, pulled out his phone, and took a handful of photos. "Holy crap, that's the funniest thing I've seen in a long time!"

As Jen turned to head into her house, she realized that there was a delicious scent wafting out from inside. She couldn't identify what it was but it smelled wonderful and her stomach growled in appreciation. She quickened her pace and headed inside. As soon as she opened the door, the flavorful scent intensified. She closed her eyes and inhaled deeply, certain that this was heaven, or at least it was what heaven smelled like.

Sitting on her couch was a large, muscular man wearing work boots, faded jeans, and a button-up flannel shirt. His hair was dark, short, and held just a hint of curl. His face was scattered with small, round scars, as though he had experienced a severe bout of acne as a teenager. A cutting board was perched confidently on his knees and the man busily chopped vegetables as he watched the television with half an eye. When he saw Jen, he looked up and smiled. "Hey, you're home." He spoke with a slight Mexican accent. He scraped the vegetables into a bowl and set them down on the coffee table. "Patrick said you'd been suffering from taco withdrawals so we figured we'd fix you up a feast."

Jen smiled back at him. Ignacio, more commonly referred to as Nacho, was one of Patrick's friends from work whom she had met on a couple previous occasions. Despite his brawn, Jen knew that he was almost as harmless as the average housecat. "That sounds awesome."

Jose, another friend and coworker of Patrick's, was stretched out in the Bark-O-Lounger. He tilted his head and smiled at Jen. He had a much thinner build than Nacho but there was a little bit of toned muscle barely showing through his clothing. His hair and eyes were dark and there was just a little bit of stubble on the lower half of his face. Obviously, he hadn't been able to shave that morning. "Yeah. He said you've been surviving off of fast-food tacos or something like that. You know we couldn't let that slide." His speech was only barely accented, and you could hear the smile in his voice, even if you couldn't see it.

"Nacho! You done wit' those veggies yet?" A shrill voice called out from the kitchen. "I need 'em!" Paco, the last of the trio, stepped into view, and Jen could barely contain her laughter. He was the shortest of the three, barely over five feet tall, and had by far the most pronounced accent, particularly when he got excited. His black hair was a little too long, hanging almost to his shoulders, but he had it pulled back in a low ponytail. His nose was a little too long and pointed, but his face was so animated that it was barely noticeable. He was dressed in the standard uniform of work boots, jeans, and a button-down shirt, but he had a towel wrapped around his waist to serve as an apron and held a spatula threateningly in one hand.

"Yeah, I got 'em right here," Nacho answered. He held the bowl up towards Jen. "Would you take these in to him, please?"

She took the bowl, still snickering. Paco turned back towards the stove as she approached and once he moved out of the doorway she was able to see her brother. Patrick stood next to the stove as well, stretching his hand towards one of the four skillets that Paco was tending on the stove.

Paco swatted at him with the spatula, barely missing him as Patrick pulled back. "You stay out!" he screeched at him.

"Don't tell me to stay out," Patrick said as he dropped a chunk of meat into his mouth. "I am your boss, after all."

"No," Paco responded emphatically as he took the bowl from Jen. "Outside, there you the boss. In here, I'm the boss." As if to drive his point home, he thumped Patrick on the chest with his spatula. "You wanna eat, you get out."

Jen stepped forward and leaned towards the stove, basking in the aroma of whatever he was cooking. Strips of seasoned meat sizzled in one pan, peppers, onions, other colorful vegetables and spices sautéed in another. A third pan held a black bean mixture, and a fourth held nothing more than oil, heated almost to a boil. "What's that one for?" she asked, stepping back quickly so as to not get swatted by Paco's spatula.

"That's for the tortillas, of course."

Jen was confused, but only until she discovered that Patrick had actually been working in the kitchen, not just pestering Paco. He had a bowl of cornmeal dough on one of the counters and a small machine plugged into the wall. As she watched, he scooped a small amount of the dough out of the bowl and put it into the round griddle inside the machine. When he closed the lid, a little green light lit up on the outside of the lid. "Not quite the traditional way to make them," he explained to Jen, "but it's a lot faster and easier to do in a small space." When the green light turned off, he opened the lid and pulled out a fresh, homemade tortilla.

Once Paco decided the oil was hot enough, he took the stack of tortillas that Patrick had made and, one by one, slipped them into the pan. As they bubbled and roiled in the hot oil, he shaped them into taco shells.

As Jen watched him cook, she noticed a small bowl in her windowsill. Next to the bowl was a shot glass that was filled with a rich, amber-colored liquid. When she leaned forward to see what it was, Paco pulled her back with one of the fourteen hands he must have grown to maneuver that many things on the stove and still have one free to restrain her. "That's for the spirits, you can leave it be."

He scooped a small bit of the vegetable mix out of the pan and set it gently in the bowl. "I think homemade offerings are a lot better than those cheap things everybody sells in the stores. You never know what's in those." He shook his head. "Can't trust 'em, that's for sure."

When all the food was cooked, everyone

gathered at the kitchen table. Paco, Patrick, and Troy carried out dish after dish of delicious smelling food and everyone had a good laugh as Paco swatted Troy for dipping into the meal before it was served.

Paco was stern, even outside the kitchen at the dinner table. A few times during the meal, he swatted Patrick for having his elbows on the table and even reached out once to thump Troy for reaching across the table instead of asking for something to be passed over to him. "You have manners!" He growled at the hybrid when Troy tried to protest. "You a guest here like we are."

Troy pulled his hand back and held it to his chest. "You had a grandmother that beat you over your table manners, didn't you?"

Paco nodded. "Looks like you could have used one too."

He had made far too much for the small group that was there, so everyone was able to eat their fill. There was even enough left over that Jose and Patrick loaded every container they could find with the food and stuffed the refrigerator full.

"Hey, check it out, Jen," Patrick called over to her once they were finished. "There's actually food in your fridge!"

After the last of the mess was cleaned up and Jose and Troy finished washing the dishes, with plenty of complaining to be had from Troy, everybody settled into the living room with cups of coffee to watch the evening movie.

As Jen drifted off to sleep that night, she had to admit that she felt a lot better than she had in a while. She wasn't sure whether it was due to the amazing meal she had eaten, the amusement of watching the guys argue over dinner, or just being around so many people who were obviously happy and content no matter where they were. Whichever it was, she didn't care.

If only every day could be like that, she mused to herself as she fell asleep.

Far too soon, her alarm went off. With a groan, she rolled over just enough to hit the snooze button so that she could sleep for just a couple more precious minutes. The last thing she wanted to do was get out of bed but she didn't exactly have a choice. She had to be at the office in less than two hours and she needed to wake up before heading out or she'd never survive the drive.

When the alarm went off for the third time, she sighed and rolled out of bed. "I wonder if I can call in tired," she mused to herself as she stumbled towards her closet. As she pulled out her last clean uniform, she reminded herself, not for the first time, that she really needed to do some laundry. The point was really driven home when she went to her dresser to pull out a pair of socks and discovered she had none. Grimacing to herself, she looked down at the pile of dirty clothes, knelt next to it, and hoped she could find a pair that weren't too awful.

Finally dressed, she headed out in search of coffee, thankful that she had finally remembered to set the timer on the coffee maker. She poured a cup to help her start waking up and dug through the cupboard, looking for her go-mug. Somehow, she knew that she would need a bit more coffee than usual to get her feet under her.

Troy and Patrick were still in the middle of their nightly snore wars, so she left them to sleep. Just because she had to be up at the break of dawn didn't mean that they had to be punished as well. Besides, she told herself, Troy had wanted to go out and enjoy the holiday and there was no reason for him not to. If she woke him now, he would just spend the day bored, knowing he was missing out on all the fun.

Sipping at her coffee, she rummaged in the fridge, pulling out a handful of cartons and the leftover tortillas that hadn't been turned into taco shells. She spread a few of the tortillas out on the counter and began scooping leftovers into them. Once they were all pretty much stuffed, she scattered some shredded cheese over each of them and rolled them into burritos.

She spent a moment drinking the last of her coffee and looking around the kitchen for something to put the burritos in. As she refilled her cup, she remembered a long-forgotten roll of aluminum wrap somewhere in her cupboards. A quick search revealed the package hidden behind a few boxes of breakfast cereal. She pulled out a few sheets of the foil and wrapped her burritos in them, satisfied that even if she was busy at lunchtime, she wouldn't go hungry. Even a cold burrito was better than no burrito, in her opinion.

After shoving her foil-wrapped lunch into a plastic bag, she poured the last of the coffee into her travel mug and headed out the door. She checked her watch as she climbed into the Jeep. "Plenty of time," she mused to herself.

Although lunch was taken care of, coffee would not be enough to sustain her until it was consumed. She stopped at her favorite break-fast place, a drive-through restaurant that car-ried fifteen different varieties of coffee, twice that many types of Danishes and muffins, and strips of deep-fried French toast sticks that were made with syrup in the batter and came dusted with powdered sugar. There was an op-tion of getting a little packet of jelly to dip them in as well but Jen preferred to eat them as they were, straight out of the box.

When she arrived at the office, she was sur-prised to find out that she was only the second member of the team to arrive. She walked into the team's meeting room carrying her bag of burritos, a box that held her last three French toast sticks, two Danishes, and a muffin, the cup of coffee that she had gotten with her breakfast, and her travel mug. She looked at Marc with one eyebrow raised as she set it all down on one of the tables. "What? Breakfast is the most important meal of the day, isn't it?"

Marc simply snickered and shook his head. "I wasn't expecting you to be the first one here. I thought you weren't a morning person."

"I'm not," she answered as she pulled out another toast stick. "Technically, you were the first one her. But it sounded like it was important for us to all be here on time today."

Marc nodded approvingly. "Yeah, today's a pretty important day, that's for sure."

They sat and chatted for a few minutes, waiting for everyone else to arrive. Slowly the rest of the team filtered in, most of them carrying lunches and cups of coffee. Everyone looked groggy except for Mike, who looked far too chipper for anyone's taste.

Jen had the sneaking suspicion that Mike was one of those strange creatures known as morning people. This wasn't the first time he had appeared far too alert in the morning and she just hoped that he wasn't the advanced form of morning person, one who hit the gym or went jogging before the rest of the world was even out of bed.

Everyone was dressed and prepared in their gear, set and ready to go, but for now there was nowhere to go to. They all knew that they would be hanging out at the office and waiting for a report of suspicious activity to filter down that would require their response but until then all they could do was to stay alert and keep themselves occupied. Marc seemed to be the only one who had been prepared for the wait; he pulled out a deck of cards and started to shuffle them. "Who's in for a poker game?"

Everyone immediately congregated at his table, pulling chairs over so that they could play. Soon, there was a lively game going and the time moved much more quickly.

Every half hour, Marc would check in with David by calling his office. These phone calls served as more than just markers of time, they also reassured the team that they weren't waiting there for nothing and that there really was someone keeping an eye out for suspicious activity.

"What if nothing happens?" Jen finally asked Marc after his fourth phone call. "Do we just sit here until midnight and waste the whole day?"

Marc laughed at her question. "I wish. Don't worry, something's going to happen and I'll bet it happens long before midnight."

"Why are you so sure?"

"Because it's the Festival of Souls," he explained simply. "And it never fails, people who have a little bit of power always believe that they have more control over it than they actually do and they try to do something beyond their natural ability level. Because there is so much power, and so much booze, flowing out there, people think that they can use the extra power to bolster their own. With so many people doing something stupid, *someone* is bound to succeed."

Jen nodded. "That makes sense, I guess." It also made sense that the longer the day went, the more alcohol would be consumed. That alcohol consumption would almost inevitably be followed by poor, if not downright dangerous, life choices on the part of the intoxicated. "But what if we're not the ones that get called?"

"Chances are, there'll be more than one incident today. Worst case, we get called out on something stupid and it's easy for us to take care of. But no matter what happens, we all get a nice day's worth of active pay."

The rest of the team toasted that and Ty dealt out a new hand of poker.

# Chapter 5

After almost four and a half hours of waiting and playing poker to pass the time, the game started to get old. When Marc's phone rang, everyone perked up and turned to hear what was happening, ready to do something, anything, to break the boredom. Even Marc brightened as he spoke. "Where was that? Okay. We're on our way."

Jen couldn't hear the rest of the conversation but it didn't matter. The team was finally rolling out and she was ready to go. She picked up her shotgun from the table next to the door where it had been waiting along with the rest of the team's large weapons and stepped into the elevator. Within seconds she was joined by the rest of the team, all of them fueled by the anticipation and buzzing with excitement.

Marc had the directions to the incident site, so all of them followed him. Much as she detested riding with other people, Jen had to settle for riding with J.J. because she wasn't allowed to take her Jeep out on official responses. As they pulled out of the quiet parking garage where the New World trucks were stored, however, she became very glad that she wasn't driving.

The streets were a mess, filled with partygoers and flying streamers, confetti, and debris everywhere. People wandered out into the street, seemingly oblivious of the vehicles that were barreling down towards them. As J.J. slammed on his brakes in an attempt to avoid a group of drunken revelers that stumbled out in front of them, Jen held on to the dashboard, praying that the truck's brakes continued to work efficiently. While she regularly maintained her own vehicle to ensure the safety of herself and any passengers she may have, she had no such confirmation about the maintenance of the New World vehicles.

She could tell when they got close to the

incident site. The intoxicated masses were still everywhere but some appeared to be running out of the area with more of a sense of purpose and she got the very real impression that these people were running for their lives. Unable to go any further due to the crowds, J.J. parked the truck in the middle of the street and stepped out. "Looks like we're walking from here."

Jen hopped out as well and pulled her shotgun out with her. Rather than shouldering it by its sling as she generally would, she felt that it would be more prudent to hold it in her hands, keeping it ready for whatever threat lay ahead.

The rest of the team parked in a similar manner and as a group they headed into the fray. The only person to stay behind was Marc. Because of his broken leg, there was no way he could maneuver through the crowd and if the team needed to move in a hurry, he would quickly become a liability. "I'll wait here with the trucks," he called out to the group. "If you need me to send in backup, let me know and I can have another team called in. I'm sure there's more in the area."

Everybody was bumped and jostled as they

worked their way through the panicked crowd. They kept close to each other, knowing without having to be told that if anyone fell in a crowd like that, there was a very real chance that they could be trampled to death before anyone could pull them back to their feet.

Finally, the crowd thinned and they were able to have a look around. There were remnants of an outdoor party, with chairs and tables of food everywhere. Off to one side, a stereo played electronic dance music, which seemed drastically out of place considering the carnage that had become of the party. Everything they saw appeared to be from a normal backyard block party, with the exception of the human wreckage that drew everyone's immediate attention.

Countless bodies were scattered across the ground. A number of them appeared as though they had been stabbed and clawed by a large, sharp weapon and a few bodies appeared to have been partially dismembered. Pieces of the unfortunate partiers lay scattered about and the ground was slick with their blood.

Far on the other side of the carnage, the team could hear screaming. Unlike the excited shouting that the crowd had been doing, these screams held much more fear. There were no words, just the wailing of agony mixed with terror.

The group took off towards the sound, trying not to slip and fall in the bloodbath or trip over bodies of those who had already been killed. Jen took a second longer to get moving than the rest of the group had, shocked by the chaos and carnage before her. Although she had heard about Festival parties getting out of control and resulting in injuries, even the occasional death, she hadn't ever heard of anything this extreme. She wondered if this kind of thing happened every year, or if something exceptional had happened. She quickly caught up with the others as they passed behind a small copse of trees.

There, they found the source of the screams.

Two enormous people in dark armor were there, each at least ten feet tall and almost four feet wide. Each wore a full plate of armor, much like the dashing knights in fairy tales would wear, but these were black as the night itself and glistening with the blood of their victims.

One of the knights, who had a red fringe of hair running from its faceplate to the back of its neck, held a young man aloft, gripping the screaming man by his legs in one hand and his head in the other. The other knight, this one with a crest of blue on its helmet, held a young woman not much older than Jen with one arm in each hand. In unison, as though by some unseen and unheard signal, both of the knights began to pull on their prisoners, ripping joints out of socket with no expression of remorse.

"What the hell?" J.J. exclaimed in surprise at the sight. "What are those?" Even as he questioned what he was seeing, he called back to Marc to report what they had encountered. If their team ended up requiring backup, it would be better if those who came to assist knew what to expect.

As the screams of the young pair intensified, Jen couldn't just stand where she was and watch. Without thinking, she ran towards the closest armored giant, intent on distracting it even if she couldn't stop it outright. She debated for only a second before lifting her shotgun. As the round exploded against the black knight's armor, she hoped that she hadn't hit its victim with any of the shrapnel. Although she had aimed well away from the now-silent man, the spread pattern of the shotgun's ammunition was hard to determine.

"Ah, hell," Mike responded. "Are those things even human?"

On the other hand, Jen decided, she didn't care. If winging one of the knights' victims with part of her shot helped to keep them both alive, she was all for the idea. As the behemoth turned towards her, she took some satisfaction in seeing that it had released some of the tension on its victim.

With a feral grin, she racked another round into her gun. If one shot got its attention, she reasoned, two shots might just do the trick.

"Jen!" She heard Ty's voice call out from behind her. "Move to your right."

Without turning to acknowledge her teammate, she took a step to her right, hoping that was far enough for him to get a clear shot. At the same time as she moved, the blue-fringed knight tossed its victim to the ground, narrowly missing Jen where she now stood. The man crumpled in a heap where he landed, making no move to get out of the area.

"He alive?" Ty called out.

Jen hoped for a brief moment that he was just unconscious, but considering that the knight had been yanking on him by the head, and the unnatural position his head was in, she realized how unlikely that was. "Doesn't look like it," she responded. Although training dictated that she should physically confirm the man's status, there wasn't much point.

The absurdity of the entire scene truly struck home as she noted how the gentle breeze that flowed through the area seemed to caress the fallen man's hair, as though easing him in his last moments. The sounds of the terrified partygoers, already distant as they had been fleeing the area, sounded even further away now, as though they were muffled somehow.

Far more important than the wind and the terrified victims was the next sound she heard, one that was swiftly closing in on Jen and her team. The sound seemed familiar, but she couldn't immediately identify it.

Before she was able to get off another shot,

the now-recognizable sound of canine howls echoed through the area. Three of the biggest dogs Jen had ever seen came barreling through the trees towards them. One of them slammed directly into J.J. and knocked him over. The beast kept running, leaving enormous, muddy paw prints up J.J.'s back as it went. All three of the dogs stopped just before reaching the black knights and turned to face Jen and her team, teeth bared, haunches lowered, and growling menacingly.

"You okay?" Mike called over.

"Yeah," J.J. grunted as he pushed himself back to his feet.

Each dog was about four feet tall at the shoulder, with shaggy grey and brown mottled fur, black eyes, and long, sharp fangs and claws. Their movements were quick and direct, without much wasted movement, and to Jen, they reminded her of the stories her grandfather used to tell of the hounds that belonged to hell itself.

Jen took two swift steps backward to move away from the closest dog, which had insinuated itself between her and the blue-fringed knight. Once both of the dogs were in place between the knights and the humans, the red-fringed knight threw the woman he had been toying with to the ground and both knights turned in unison to walk away. Mike ran towards the woman, dodging around the closest dog. He swept her up over his shoulder and carried her back behind the rest of the group, where he carefully laid her on the ground.

"Marc, we're gonna need medical to roll in here," Ty called out over the radio. "We've got who knows how many dead and two injured, possibly badly."

"Pretty sure this one's dead," Jen called over her shoulder. "Looks like a broken neck."

"Copy that," Marc's voice came from everyone's radio, giving the sound a surreal quality. "Are you guys okay?"

"Yeah, we're fine," Ty responded. "But we've got a handful of unknowns in here. Looks like a couple of black knights and some hellhounds. We've got them, so go ahead and get medical rolling. We'll call you when it's clear for them to come in."

"Got it. I'm calling them now."

"So how do we want to handle this?" Jen looked around at the rest of the group. "We can't just let them leave, so it looks like we're going to have to get past these first." She indicated the dogs, which were still blocking the area between them and the black knights. None of the gigantic dogs had moved from their guard positions, not even when Mike had moved in to grab the woman. They didn't seem intent on attacking the response team but that could change without warning, as they all well understood.

J.J. answered with actions, not with words. He drew his shotgun and leveled it at the closest hellhound. With a quick pull of the trigger, the slug ripped into the dog's shoulder.

It howled and stepped back, limping a bit as it moved, but to everyone's surprise, it didn't fall down. Instead, it moved its head down to lick at its wound, dropping pieces of the shell onto the blood-covered ground.

Jen didn't wait to see if the vile creatures actually were capable of healing themselves. Deciding that J.J. had the right idea, she fired a shot at the closest dog to her, racked another round, and fired again. The sounds of her gunshots were quickly joined by more as the rest of the team opened fire as well. Pistol, rifle, and shotgun rounds flew at the dogs and at the armored figures beyond them.

At that moment, Jen was pretty sure that she would have given just about anything to have one of Troy's explosives with her. Why did she leave him asleep at home again? She wondered to herself.

Finally, the team's firestorm began to have a visible effect on the dogs. One of them fell outright, landing with a ground-shaking thud onto its stomach as its legs collapsed. It struggled to stand again but couldn't quite manage to push itself back up. Seeing this, the other two hellhounds began to retreat in the direction from where the knights had disappeared.

The team moved forward cautiously, not trusting that the fallen creature would stay down or that they weren't moving into a trap. Ty stepped up directly in front of the fallen beast, put the barrel of his shotgun against the front of the massive creature's skull, and fired one more shot. With barely a twitch, the beast fell, this time for good.

As sounds of more violence came from up ahead, the team moved quickly to see where the knights and their dogs had gone. J.J. called back to Marc as they moved. "We're moving to another location. We still need medical for the wounded people, but there's still a hellhound, possibly dead, at this location, and we are in pursuit of the others."

"Okay. I'll have the medical team move in with an escort. What's the status of the possibly dead target?"

"I'm not sure. It may have been neutralized, but we didn't have time to make sure. If medical comes in, make sure they've got a damn good guard with them."

The group caught back up with the knights and their dogs on the main street once more. There, they discovered that the knights had climbed onto gigantic black horse-like creatures. The mounts resembled oversized Clydesdales, with glossy black fur and long, thick, mottled, snake-like tails. They had elongated, predatory snouts, with oversized nostrils and the pointed teeth of carnivores. One of them snorted and pawed at the ground as it saw the group.

Once mounted, the knights and the two remaining hellhounds moved into the crowd of people. They turned towards a group of partiers, who were obviously drunk and confused and seemed to think that the mounted killers were all a show for the Festival. The partiers cheered and clapped, continuing to celebrate right up until the enormous mounts plowed into them. Some of the partygoers were left wounded, with large gashes in their arms, legs, or torsos, but a handful of them were killed immediately. One of the less fortunate ones had his head torn almost completely off as one of the horses grabbed his hair and the top of his head in its teeth and then stepped on the body as it walked over him. It tugged as it walked and the crunch of breaking bones seemed to sober up a few of the other people who were gathered.

The people screamed and panicked, trying to run away from the bloodthirsty beasts, but space in the roadway was limited and the knights, their mounts, and the dogs took up much room so that one or more was everywhere the people turned. More fell, trampled beneath the cloven hooves of the mounts as they made their way through the group.

Jen's team fired more shots at the monstrous creatures, but most were deflected by the knights' armor. In desperation, J.J. pulled out his net launcher and fired it at one of the behemoths.

The net flew perfectly and quite clearly demonstrated the amount of time J.J. spent training with it. It sailed over the knight with the red-fringed helmet's head and settled down around its shoulders. The bolas on the edges of the net clinked against the armor as it restricted and the knight gave a yowl, the first vocalization from either of them, as it struggled to free itself from the restraint. The sound was hollow and strangely metallic, as though it was the armor itself making the noise instead of whatever type of being was inside it.

For a moment, Jen wondered whether there was even a living creature inside either of the knights at all. She quickly shook the thought from her mind, however. How could a set of armor become animated, after all?

Taking his cue from J.J., Mike launched his net at the blue-fringed knight, with similar results. As the pair struggled to free themselves, Ty and Jen each fired on the dogs, hoping to end the carnage quickly.

While Jen's net snared the dog she had been aiming for, Ty's target moved so that it was no longer within range to be hit by the net. The knight with the red fringe wrestled an arm free, doubled back on his mount, and reached down to scoop up the hapless dog, netting and all. The other knight ignored the netting completely and spurred his mount, which quickly stepped up into a gallop. Within seconds, the knight was gone from view and the other knight and both dogs were close behind.

The team tried to give chase but quickly realized that it was futile. The knights moved much more quickly and had already gotten too far ahead for them to have any hope of catching up.

"Marc, we're going to need medical at our current location," Mike called in. "I have no idea how many here are dead or how many are wounded. Either way, there's a lot of both."

"Got that," Marc replied. "The medical team's almost done with the two in the last area, so I'll send 'em up your way as soon as they're finished."

"Okay. We're gonna head back that way now, too. We'll stop and pick up the target from the last area on the way."

"Got it. What about the other targets you were chasing? Where are they?"

Mike sighed. "They got away; we couldn't catch up."

On the other end of the radio, Marc was silent for a long moment. "Okay," he finally responded. "I'll see you when you get back." Even over the radio, the disappointment was clearly discernable.

The group turned to head back the way they had come. The giant dog that they had taken down still lay motionless, exactly where they had left it. It looked dead but Mike wasn't in any mood to take chances. He wrapped a couple lengths of rope around the enormous creature and dragged it back towards Marc and the trucks.

As they walked, they passed the medical crew that Marc had called in. There were four paramedics and a good dozen police with them for security. Ty stopped to talk with them for a couple of minutes, describing the carnage in the next area, before they continued on once more.

Back out at the trucks, Marc was still waiting where they had left him. "What the hell happened in there?" he called out to them as soon as they were in view. "I thought you were going to take care of the threat, not just chase it off."

"We tried," Mike grunted as he pulled the enormous canine into view. "But they had more backup than we expected."

Marc took a step backwards as Mike dropped the dog in front of him. "What the hell is that?"

"Mean," Ty supplied. "Vicious and mean, that's what it is." He helped Mike heave the creature into the back of Marc's truck. "We thought you'd want a souvenir."

"That's the creature that did all the damage?"

Marc asked as he watched the men tie down the animal.

"Nope," Ty growled as he tightened one of the straps. "This is a pet of the creatures that did all this."

"Pet?"

"Something like that, yeah. These things weren't even there when we arrived; I have no idea where they came from."

Marc nodded. "Okay." He looked around at the crowd, which hadn't thinned out much since their arrival. "Let's get this thing back to the office. From there, we can call the NPIB and see if they have any ideas."

The National Paranormal Investigative Board was the governmental agency that oversaw all paranormal activity in the country. Each region had their own section of the department and all response companies answered to the NPIB. They sent out orders, authorized non-emergency activities, and approved or denied all certification applications for response team members.

Beyond all that, the NPIB also controlled one of the biggest databases on paranormal activity in the world. Over the last fifty years or so, the NPIB had compiled information on all paranormal actions in the country, both legitimate and faked. If there was a creature that had been reported anywhere in the last fifty years, or longer if there were accurate enough records, it was in the NPIB database.

They took the long way back to the office, scouting the area for any sign that the black knights and their hounds had passed through. After over forty minutes of circling and searching, there was still no sign of their quarry. With no further options at their disposal, they headed back to the office.

Jen was thoroughly displeased with the entire affair. She felt that the black knights would continue to cause havoc and damage wherever they were and that if they weren't stopped, and soon, there would be no telling how many people would end up dead. There was no point in trying to explain this to anyone else in the team, however, because she could tell that they all felt the same way she did.

She just wished that there was more they could do.

Back at the office, Ty and Mike untied the creature from the back of Marc's truck and hauled it over to a small storage shed that Jen hadn't noticed before. Before opening the shed, they took a couple dozen photographs of the animal from all different directions. Once they were finished, they dragged the beast inside the shed and secured the door with a pair of sturdy padlocks before heading inside the office.

David was waiting for them just inside the doors. "I hear you had a bit of trouble out there," he said as they walked into the building. "Is everybody all right?"

"Yeah, we're fine," J.J. grumbled in response. "Just a bit tired and pissed off, I think."

David nodded. "I believe it." He looked down at the camera in Ty's hand. "You got the pictures?"

"Of course," he answered and handed over the camera. "I just hope you find something useful about these things because they're damn hard to kill."

"Let's hope so." He slipped the camera into a pocket and looked the group over. "Why don't you guys go get cleaned up and grab a bite to eat? I'll call you if anything pops up."

Everyone thought that was a pretty good idea, so they headed for the elevator to head down to the team room.

Downstairs, Jen headed straight for her mug of coffee, which she had forgotten at the table in her haste to leave earlier. The coffee inside was cold but she didn't care. It was caffeine and that was all that mattered. Once her cup was empty, she took her bag of burritos over to the microwave.

Mike stopped her before she started the microwave. "What are you doing?"

"Heating up my lunch," she answered. "I'm starving."

"Not like that, you aren't." He caught the door to the microwave before she was able to close it all the way. "You can't put that in the microwave."

"Why not?" She looked at the wrapped burritos, and realization dawned. "Oh, dammit, I didn't even think of that." Her burritos were still wrapped in the aluminum sheets. She pulled them back out of the microwave and proceeded to unwrap them. "Thanks."

"Purely selfish reasons," he teased her as he stuck his meal in the microwave and started it. "I just wanted to get my food before you blew up the micro."

Jen snickered in response as she put her burritos on a paper napkin. Leave it to Mike to lighten the mood, she thought to herself. The guy could crack a joke about anything.

After he was done, Jen was finally able to heat up her lunch and get a fresh cup of coffee from the pot that J.J. had so thoughtfully started. She was pleased that she even managed to sneak up to the pot and get a cup before J.J. had been able to get his.

They waited at the office, eating, reloading their weapons, and generally cleaning up as much as they could while they waited for either word about where the black knights had gone or another assignment. Slowly, they started to calm down, even managing to get back into their poker game after a brief argument over who had taken their turn last and who still had to toss in their bets.

Jen had a harder time relaxing than she let on, however. She couldn't shake the sight of the horse-creature decapitating one of the men on the street. She wasn't sure whether that was worse than watching the knights as they prepared to rip the people apart when she and the rest of the group arrived on the scene. She was fairly certain that it was worse, because at least one of the others had survived. But the callous way the knights had held their victims, as though tearing people apart was some sort of a game to them, shook her far more than she was willing to admit. She pulled the token that Sahara had made her promise to carry with her from her pocket and toyed with it as she thought.

Only a couple hours later, Marc's phone rang again. Everyone turned to watch as he answered the call. "It's a what? Yeah, I think we can handle that." He paused for a moment, listening. "No, I can do it, I'll be fine. Okay, we're on our way."

As he hung up the phone, Ty asked, "Did they find them?" Apprehension showed on his face as he asked. Although all of them would be willing to go back out after the black knights, none of them were eager.

Marc shook his head. "This is something different. Apparently there's a poltergeist that's picked a fight with some partiers. They just want us to go break it up and calm everyone down before it gets out of hand."

Once again, everyone grabbed their gear and headed up to the parking garage, much more subdued this time than they had been the last time they had responded to a call. Within minutes, they were back out on the streets, fighting to get where they needed to be without running over anybody in the process.

If anything, the crowds had only gotten worse since they were last outside.

"Damn, I hate the Festival," J.J. grumbled as he swerved to miss a stumbling group of drunk teenagers. "It's like common sense goes straight out the window. I mean, look at those ones, I'd bet that none of them are old enough to be drinking. If I'd come home that drunk after Festival, my dad would've kicked my ass." He grinned. "And that's only if my granny didn't beat him to it," he snickered.

Jen nodded. "I remember one year my brother Todd and I went out partying with a group of our friends and a couple of them had brought some alcohol. We thought it'd be a lot of fun, so we downed every bit we could. Five teen-agers and two bottles of rum, I don't think I've been that drunk since."

He let out a low whistle. "That's a lot of alcohol. What happened?"

"Mom saw us on the parade coverage. I don't remember it, but apparently we wanted to ride on one of the floats. So, we went down to the parade route and just climbed onto one of them. I don't even remember which one it was but I guess it was all over the news that night."

J.J. burst out laughing. "I bet your parents loved that one."

"Oh, yeah. I have no idea how we got home that night; they may have picked us up from the police station for all I know. But I do re-member waking up the next morning, next to Todd. We were both hanging upside down off a wall in the living room, covered in duct tape from toes to hips."

"You're kidding," J.J. looked over at her in surprise.

Jen shook her head. "Nope, dad said that it was in case we threw up, so that we wouldn't choke on it. He had plastic, some sort of tarp or maybe trash bags, I really don't remember, covering the floor beneath us."

"That sounds awful."

"Oh, yeah. That was the worst hangover I've ever had. Whether it was that bad because I hadn't ever been drunk before or because I was upside down, I have no idea."

He was still snickering when they pulled up to a stop behind Marc. This time, they were able to pull off to the side of the road to park so they didn't have to leave someone behind to stay with the trucks.

As the group gathered on the sidewalk, they could easily see where the disturbance was happening. Food, thrown high into the air, rained down on the crowd. A number of onlookers had turned their attention away from the party in the streets in order to watch the action unfolding off to the side. Many of the spectators were cheering, and a howl raised from the crowd as more fruit sailed over them.

Jen and the team elbowed their way through the gathered masses, working towards the center of the crowd. There, they found a partially-corporeal poltergeist and a young man, standing about ten feet apart and facing each other. The poltergeist had a muffin in one hand and an apple in the other while the human had a golf club and seemed to be encouraging the spirit to throw something at him.

"Come on," he motioned with one hand as he spoke, "right over the plate."

The poltergeist threw the muffin at the man, who swung the golf club like a baseball bat. Shreds of muffin sailed over the crowd, causing another cheer to explode from the spectators.

"Troy?" Jen stepped closer to have a better look at the man wielding the golf club. "What the hell are you doing?"

Distracted, Troy lowered his makeshift bat to look over at her. "Jen? When did you get here?"

The poltergeist used the distraction to

bounce the apple off of Troy's chest. With a grunt, the hybrid looked back over at the spirit. "Hey, come on," he protested. "I was distracted, that didn't count!"

The poltergeist grinned and looked around for another piece of food to throw at him. Members of the crowd gleefully offered up bits of fruit, breads, and Jen even spotted one that was trying to hand over half a sandwich. "Oh, come on, Patrick, why are you encouraging this?"

Patrick just grinned as the spirit took his offered sandwich. As the poltergeist wound up for another pitch, Jen turned back to her team. "I think we're okay here. The only person the spirit seems to be picking on is that idiot over there and believe me, he deserves every bit of it."

# Chapter 6

That night, Jen had a hard time getting to sleep. The horror that the black knights had inflicted during the Festival haunted her and she couldn't get the images of the people they had killed out of her head. Shortly before four in the morning, she gave up and headed out in search of coffee.

In the living room, she found Patrick and Troy, both sleeping off the previous day's revelry. When she had left the previous morning, she had let them both sleep in the hopes that they would enjoy themselves. From what she had seen of their activities she was certain they had done exactly that. In the kitchen, she pulled the tin of coffee out of the cupboard. As she went to put it down on the counter so she could scoop some into the filter basket, the tin slipped from her hands. The lid popped off as it hit the linoleum and coffee grounds spilled across the floor. With a sigh, she walked to the closet to pull out the broom and dustpan, thankful that she hadn't woken the sleeping men in the next room.

Once she finished cleaning up the mess, she realized that she couldn't salvage enough coffee from what was left in the tin to make a pot. She put her cleaning supplies away and headed for her bedroom to get dressed.

Again, she reminded herself that she needed to do laundry, and she made a halfhearted effort to sort the clothes into piles as she got dressed. Not trusting that any of the socks in the pile were reusable, she decided to go without. One day without socks shouldn't kill her.

When she was dressed, she headed outside. Rather than driving down to the little corner market, she decided to walk. After all, it was only a couple blocks away so walking shouldn't be any problem.

Moonlight and streetlamps eased their way through the thin, early morning fog as Jen walked. She looked around in amazement as the fog softened the edges of everything and obscured some of the buildings at the end of her street. The few lights she could see up ahead were large fuzzy globes of color and all of the sounds around her were muted noises, barely audible as she walked.

The entire world felt so silent that she could almost believe that she was the only person left, that some strange catastrophe had happened and the rest of the population had disappeared. Even her own footfalls sounded muffled, as though the mist that surrounded her had padded the sidewalk beneath her feet. She shook the idea from her head as soon as it appeared, however, and reminded herself that it was just the weather playing tricks on her mind, combined with not enough sleep and not enough coffee.

Soon enough, the familiar lights of the Speedy Mart shone ahead. Almost unconsciously, Jen sped up her pace to make it inside quickly. The electronic bell that sounded as she stepped through the door was a welcome change from the dull silence that had surrounded her since leaving her house. Gentle music flowed from hidden speakers and the scent of freshly made donuts filled the room. "Oh, good, you got your delivery already," she sighed.

She almost headed straight for the donut display but then remembered that she had priorities. She redirected towards the coffee stand and poured herself twenty-four ounces worth of deliciously scented and flavored caffeine.

Once she had her cup of liquid life and was able to take a couple of deep drinks from the hot, spicy brew, she turned back towards the donut display. She pulled out a small box from a pocket on the side of the glass case and unfolded it as she perused the selection. Maple bars, chocolate bars, plain glazed old-fashioned circles, and so many more choices faced her that she quickly decided that the best choice she could make was no choice at all. Instead, she pulled out two of each type of donut. That way, she figured, if the guys back home took a couple of her breakfast deliciousness, there would still be plenty there for her.

"You're in early this morning, aren't you?"

Douglas, the night clerk, stepped around the counter towards her. "Rough night?"

"You could say that," she answered as she put the box down on the checkout counter next to a small tin of coffee. "Yesterday was just a bit much for me, I guess."

Douglas nodded as he peeked into the box. "Well, I guess there's a cure for bad day syndrome in here somewhere." He chuckled as he rang her purchases in. "Oh!" He looked up in surprise. "There was something new that we got in the other day, I was going to show you."

"What's that?" She followed him across the store, where he pointed to a small display of key chains.

"These are new, and I immediately thought of you when they came in." He picked up one of the key chains and showed how the fob had a small button on it that turned on the built-in flashlight. "And here's another that has a pen attached, so you always have one handy." He handed her a keychain that had a pen that was less than two inches long attached to it and stood back, smiling, as she checked out the toys.

"These are pretty cool," she agreed as she picked out one of each. "I can actually use them, too."

"I know; that's why I thought of you when they came in with the last delivery. I knew you'd love them."

She took the pair of key chains back to the checkout counter. Douglas dropped them into a small plastic bag after scanning them, explaining, "I figured you'd need another trash bag for the Jeep by now."

"That's true," she agreed as she swiped her card. "I haven't changed that in over a week, thanks for reminding me." She looked back up at him. "Speaking of which, can I get some quarters back? I need to get some laundry done before all my clothes get up and walk out on me."

"Sure, no problem." He handed her the change and her receipt and held up the box of donuts so that she could get her hands underneath it.

On the walk home, Jen noticed that the fog had thickened in the short time she had spent in the store. Even the streetlights directly above her were partially obscured by the thick haze and the moon was completely invisible. She could only see about halfway down the block and almost immediately she had the feeling that she was being watched.

"Todd, I hope that's you," she whispered into the silent night.

Jen's twin brother Todd lived on the east coast but that didn't stop him from keeping an eye on his sister. A fairly powerful mage in his own right, he had spells that allowed him to literally see what she was up to at any point in time. Years ago, when Jen had first discovered his habit of spying on her, she had been furious at the invasion. Lately, however, her attitude had changed. Knowing that he was out there watching her back gave her an added sense of security because she knew that no matter what happened, Todd would always be there for her.

She still hid a small amount of jealousy that Todd had magical talent and she didn't. As children, when Todd had begun to display signs of his talent, their parents had been so proud of both of them. Everyone had assumed that Jen would turn out to have the talent as well but the months of rigorous testing that she had undergone, searching for even the smallest hint of magical ability, had turned up nothing.

Even though her parents had tried to convince her that she was still special in her own right, things had never been the same after that. She and Todd were still twins, still extremely close even for siblings, but now there was something between them that they couldn't share. For the first time in her life, Jen had to face the realization that Todd had a whole world that she couldn't be a part of. No matter how much both of them had shared up until that point, no matter how much both of them wanted to continue sharing their lives with each other, Jen simply couldn't be a part of his entire world anymore.

Being separated for the first time in their combined existence had been torture and although many years had passed since Todd had moved away to continue his training, she had only recently began getting used to the idea of living without his constant presence.

Other people's attitudes had changed also. Their parents' friends, ecstatic that they had a mage in the family, showered Todd with gifts and attention. Teachers at their school singled Todd out to let everyone know that he was a mage and he became an instant celebrity among the students. People were constantly talking about how exciting all of this was and Todd basked in the attention, but nobody seemed to notice that Jen wasn't a part of it. One of their aunts even paid for Todd to go away to a special school where his magical skill could be culti-vated and strengthened as it grew. When Todd went off to his training academy, Jen was left alone, talentless.

Even worse were the people who looked down upon Todd, telling Jen that at least she was normal, unlike her brother. At first, Jen had felt better about the attention shown to her but then she started to realize that while all they were saying was that she was normal, there was much more to the statement than just what was spoken. She stopped responding to the comments, feeling more alienated than ever before.

For a little while, she had blamed Todd, thinking that he had somehow done this on purpose. She didn't know what she had done wrong to not have any magical talent like he did, or whether she had just somehow lost hers. Briefly, she considered the possibility that Todd had somehow stolen her power during their time that they shared a womb but she soon dismissed the idea as ridiculous. Although she knew now that Todd hadn't had any more choice in his situation than she had, there were still times when pangs of resentment rose in her but she just tried her best to shove them back down where they belonged.

As her house came into view, she discovered that someone else must have woken in her absence. Lights were on in the living room and she could see a shadow move across one of the windows. Although she couldn't tell who it was from that distance, she suspected that it was Troy. He had a bad habit of raiding the fridge in the middle of the night. Considering how much leftover Mexican food there was, she had no problem letting everyone snack their way through it all.

Just so long as they left some for her, of course.

When she opened the door, Troy jumped in surprise. He had been sitting in his recliner with a plate of food on his lap and cartoons going quietly on the television. "I thought you were in bed," he said as she set the bag down on the coffee table.

"I was, but that just wasn't working out anymore."

He nodded. "Bad dreams again?"

"Yeah. The difference is, this time they aren't waiting for me to be asleep before they start."

He made a sympathetic face. "I was going to make some coffee but it looks like we're out. I can head down to the store and get some more, though."

"No need," she said as she pulled the tin from the bag. "I got it covered."

While she went into the kitchen to fire up the coffeemaker, Troy sniffed at the pastry box. "Where'd you get these?" he asked when she walked back into the room.

"At the Speedy Mart. They get fresh donuts every morning but they're usually gone by the time we hit the store." She swatted his hand away from one of the cinnamon and sugar dusted twists. "Nope, those are mine."

"Okay, no problem," he said and pulled out an apple fritter instead. He settled back into his recliner and admired the pastry. "Man, if I'd known they had donuts there, I'd have been all over that a long time ago."

Jen snickered and took a bite of her twist. It wasn't warm anymore due to her trek through the cold morning but it was still soft, chewy, and deliciously sweet. Combined with the coffee she still had left from the cup she had purchased, she decided that it just might turn out to be a good morning after all.

When Patrick woke, there were still a few donuts left for him, too. He snagged a maple bar and headed off to the shower. "I've got a meeting this morning to finalize the plans for the build," he explained as he walked down the hallway, towel over one shoulder. "So hopefully we can get going on it within the week."

Jen was happy that everything seemed to be going well for his project and she understood that this was a big one for him. If everything went according to schedule and there were no big hang-ups, he would get his next promotion, one that she knew he had been working towards for a while now. She may have been biased, but she figured that his company should have given him a dozen or so more promotions than they had already.

Later that morning, after all of the donuts were gone, the fog had lifted, and Patrick had headed off to his meeting, Jen gathered up Troy and all of the laundry to drag down to the laundromat. She would have gone on her own but Troy said he had some stuff that needed to be washed, too. They spent three hours at the laundromat, washing load after load of clothes. Twice, Jen had to run out for more change and even Troy had to go after more soap once. By the time they made it back home, Jen was exhausted. She piled all of her clothes on her bed, fell over next to them, and promptly fell asleep.

When she woke, it was dark outside and stars twinkled outside her window. She could hear noise out in the living room, so she could tell it was still early enough for the guys to be awake. She blinked at the digital clock next to her bed and realized that it was almost nine at night.

She stumbled out towards the sound, sniffing the air as she went. Either someone had cooked or they had ordered in but all she cared about was whether there was something left over for her. In the living room, she found Troy and Patrick on the edges of their seats, watching a hockey game. A stack of pizza boxes threatened to fall off the coffee table and a half-empty bottle of soda sat on the floor next to it. Without speaking, Jen sank to the floor, leaned against the couch, and pulled a slice of pepperoni pizza from the top box.

"Hey, sleeping beauty's awake," Patrick commented as the game broke for commercial. "I was just starting to think you were going to sleep through the night."

Troy snickered. "If you're sleeping beauty, does that mean Prince Charming's still back in the bedroom?"

"That'd be nice," Jen chuckled as she took another bite of pizza. "I wonder if I've been good enough to get one of those under my Yuletide tree this year."

Patrick joined in the laughter. "Ah, but you're

missing the key point there. Only *good* kids get gifts under their tree."

"Damn, I knew I'd missed something there." Jen reached over to the bottle of soda, spun off the top, and took a drink straight from the bottle. "Who's winning?" She gestured with the bottle towards the television, where the game was back on.

"The Kings," Troy answered, "by a long shot. You can barely tell the Lions are even playing."

"That bad, hmm?" Jen looked up at the screen to watch some of the action. "Strange, the Lions are usually pretty good."

"You're telling me," Troy responded. "I've got fifty bucks on this game, too. If they don't start stepping it up soon, I'm going to be pissed."

They sat, watching the last quarter of the game and eating their way through the last of the pizza until the Kings had thoroughly and completely stomped the Lions into submission. After the game ended, the news came on and Jen stopped Troy from changing the channel when he reached for the remote. As she dug through the boxes of pizza, looking for one last slice of the garlic chicken pizza, she kept half an eye on the news reports, wondering if there would be any new sightings of the black knights. She doubted it, because if there had been, she was pretty sure that she and the rest of the team would have been called in to respond to it but she still wanted to watch, just out of curiosity.

There were plenty of reports of the Festival activities, including both of the incidents that her team had responded to. There was some amusing footage of the makeshift baseball game that Troy had been involved in with the poltergeist, including a couple of good shots of the hybrid being splattered by food and one nice swing that launched what appeared to have been a partially-eaten hot dog over the crowd.

Nobody seemed to have seen the black knights since the conclusion of the Festival. That was just fine by Jen, because it meant that there was a chance that they had gone back to whichever circle of hell they had come from. However, a nagging suspicion lurked in the back of her mind that they hadn't seen the last of the knights, their foul mounts, or their evil-looking dogs.

Another report came on that caught her attention. It had nothing to do with the black knights but it still struck a chord in the back of her head. A couple of artifacts that had recently been shipped into the museum for an upcoming display had been stolen. "Police and museum personnel have refused to release which items were stolen," the reporter explained, "but they say they are still investigating."

The security cameras were disabled just before the break-in and the on-site security officers were rendered unconscious so they couldn't give any information on who had pulled off the heist. "Anyone who has any information about the break-in is encouraged to call the police department," the reporter explained at the end of the story.

Jen stayed up late again that night, not surprisingly considering how long she had slept during the day. When she wandered into the kitchen after she believed everyone was asleep, she discovered Troy, sitting at the kitchen table, sipping a beer. "Dreams again?"

"Yeah," she sighed as she pulled a bottle of water out of the fridge. "Damn, I hate this."

"Do you still have any of the stuff Sahara made for you?" The last time that Jen had been plagued by nightmares, Sahara had given her a concoction to help her sleep without dreams. It had worked perfectly, except that she had started to get midnight visits from a dreamwalker.

Jen shook her head. "I ran out of that stuff a few nights ago." She took a drink of the cold water.

"Do we need to talk to Sahara and get more?"

"No, I'll be okay. Besides, I can't go running to her every time I have a problem."

"Of course you can," Troy disagreed. "She's your best friend, that's what you're supposed to do."

Jen shook her head. "She's got enough stuff she's dealing with right now. The last thing she needs is for me to come whining to her about all this."

"Want to talk to me about it, then?" He took another swig of his beer. "I can be a pretty good listener, you know."

"I know." She sank down onto one of the chairs next to him. "And everyone says that when something's bothering you, it can help to talk about it. The problem is, I'm just not sure where to start."

Troy nodded. "It's because of those metal monsters that were on the news last night, isn't it?"

Jen looked up at him in surprise. "How could you tell?"

"Because the last time you had trouble sleeping, it was because you saw someone killed in front of you. After what they were saying on the news about what those knight things were out there doing, and since one of the videos they showed had Marc in it, it wasn't a very hard guess."

"Marc was in one of the shots? I didn't see him."

"Yep. It was only a quick shot, but I recognized him. So," he said as he reached behind him and opened the fridge. "You want to talk about it?" He pulled a bottle of beer out and slid it across the table to her. "It really does help."

"The beer, or talking?" Jen asked as she opened the bottle and took a drink.

"Both."

She sat in silence for a few minutes, sipping at her beer and gathering her thoughts. Finally, she explained about all that had happened during the Festival of Souls. She told him about the slaughter that the knights had already done before the team got there and she explained about the tug-of-war that they were about to do when she had arrived. Her voice hitched a bit as she told him about watching the horse creature rip someone's head almost completely off.

"That's the worst part," she said as she took another drink of her beer. "There was nothing I could do. We shot at them with everything we had and nothing fazed them."

Troy sat quietly as she spoke, sipping at his beer and listening sympathetically. "Believe it or not, I know how you feel," he said once she was finished. "Back when I was out in the war, there was this kid that just transferred into my unit. He was fresh out of boot, still not really sure what he was doing out there, but he was ours.

"A unit's like family. We try to look out for each other, you know?" He took another drink of his beer. "Booby trap got him. He didn't know any better. Picked up a stupid newspaper off the ground. He was just fine one second and the next, he was gone." He looked off to the side at that, and his eyes got distant. "There wasn't enough left of him to bring home.

"So, we tried to make sure that nobody was going to be putting out those booby traps anymore." A dark smirk curved his lips at the memory. "Yeah, I know helpless."

He looked back towards her. "So now we just need to figure out how to stop your problem." He took another drink of his beer, frowning as he realized his bottle was empty. He set it on the counter, reached back into the fridge, and pulled out another one. "You need one too?" He held up the bottle.

"Yeah, I could use another."

He handed the bottle over and took out one for himself. "You said these things wore armor, right?" When she nodded, he asked, "Was it made of actual metal, or do you know?"

"No, it was metal." She could still remember

some of the sparks as rounds had bounced off the armor. "Why?"

"I may have an idea; I'll just have to check on availability of parts." He cracked his beer and held it up, as if to toast. "Don't worry, though, we'll get them."

# Chapter 7

The next two days were quiet. Jen spent most of her time at the office in the basement training area. Part of it was standard training that she was required to do because all members of the team were required to have twenty hours of training logged in each month. The real reason she was there, however, was to try and burn off as much of the stress as she could. She was still kicking herself for having let the knights escape and, as much as she told herself that she couldn't have done any more to stop them, the feeling of inadequacy persisted.

Beyond just that, she knew that they hadn't heard the last of the black knights. Almost everyone else seemed to believe that their appearance was a one-day thing, but the tightly coiled knot in Jen's stomach said otherwise. She still felt guilty over how many people had already fallen to the malevolent creatures and it sickened her to think of how many more they might kill before they were stopped.

Even normally stoic Mike noticed the increased intensity of her workouts. He pulled her aside after one of their hand-to-hand training sessions. "You can't let it get to you like this," he explained. "It'll eat you from the inside and pretty soon you won't be able to do anything."

"I can't stand just sitting here and doing nothing," she said. "Those things are still out there somewhere."

"You can't know that," Mike said. "And even if they are, until we find them, there isn't anything you can do about it."

"I *do* know that." she picked up her bottle of water from the bench and took a long drink, wiping the sweat out of her eyes. "I can feel it."

"Either way, beating yourself up isn't going to bring anyone back and it isn't going to stop them, either. You can be prepared, that's fine."

He took a drink of his water as well. "In fact, that's the point of mandatory training. But if you overwork yourself now, you're going to be useless when we need you."

Not bothering to respond, Jen stomped off the showers to get cleaned up. She knew what Mike had said was true but she also knew that there was nothing else she could do until the monsters were found and stopped. The hot water burned across her sore muscles but she didn't care. She stood in the spray until everything was fogged and it was hard to see before turning the water off and climbing out.

She headed home, stopping at Taco King on the way. She hadn't stopped at Taco King, her favorite fast-food place, in a few weeks because the last time she had been there someone had tried to kill her, and not just with their super-spicy chipotle sauce. As she waited in the drive-thru to place her order, she thought back to the psychic that had attacked her the last time she had been there, dragging her car out into the street and knocking over an electric pole on top of her in the process. The pole had been repaired the following day, but her eyes still went to the scorch marks on the pavement, evidence of the attack that continued to remain.

She wondered what had happened to that psychic, because he hadn't been heard from since the attack either. Her only hope was that the psychic had been controlled by the same demon that had controlled the dreamwalker and wouldn't be a threat anymore. She wasn't sure how many more threats she could handle right then.

Once she was through the ordering line and had gotten her food, she turned towards home, hoping that after she had something to eat, she would feel better. She knew that she had been unfair to Mike, but she just hoped he wouldn't hold it against her for too long. When she got back to her house, she discovered that it was empty. Although she hadn't had the guys staying with her for too long, she had gotten used to their constant presence. She wandered through the silent house, feeling more alone than she had in a very long time. Even her monster taco supreme wasn't enough to cheer her up.

That night, when she went to bed, she hoped that she had exhausted herself enough with the workout to be able to sleep. She lay in bed for what felt like hours, staring at the ceiling and watching the shadows move across her walls. More than once, she thought she saw the frightening shape of enormous armored figures walking past her window but she managed to remind herself that it was just the trees outside, combined with her own imagination and a few too many cream-cheese filled jalapeños before bed.

Maybe asking Sahara for some more of her special concoction wasn't such a bad idea after all.

Early the next morning, she was woken by the ringing of her phone. Groggy and grouchy, she reached out to answer it. "What?"

"Jen, its Marc. We need you at the office now. There's been another incident."

Jen sat up, instantly awake. "What happened?"

"A neighborhood was attacked. I'll let you know more when you get here."

Ten minutes later, Jen walked out the door,

fully dressed and geared and ready to go. She hopped into her truck and headed towards the office, making a brief stop at a drive-through coffee kiosk along the way for her morning wake-up juice. When she got there, she was the last one to arrive, but only barely. She followed J.J. in through the door and they rode the elevator downstairs together.

In the basement, Marc and the rest of the team were already assembled and waiting. As soon as Jen and J.J. were there, Marc stared into his briefing. "This morning, the police received a report of a break-in and homicide in a suburban neighborhood towards the edge of town. When they arrived, they discovered that the residents of the house in question had all been killed. They tried to speak to the neighbors to see if anyone saw anything, but all they were able to find out was that there was more than one house in the area that was attacked.

"From the last report I got, there are over five houses in this neighborhood that were broken into. In all of these houses, the residents were found dead. Right now, the police aren't sure whether it was a human serial killer, a vampire gone rogue, or something else entirely. That's where we come in."

As the group began asking questions, Marc held up a hand for silence. "The police are still there, looking for survivors and evacuating the houses where people were found still alive. I'm not sure how long it's going to take before the media gets a hold of this but I want our team behind the police line as quickly as possible. As of right now, we don't have a final death toll, nor do we know if the culprit is still in the area. The people who are being evacuated will be checked over by the police to make sure that none of them are involved in the murders but nobody is being allowed into the zone until we give the all clear.

"The bodies of the victims are still there; the medical examiner's office legally can't take them until we've verified that this wasn't a vampire attack. As I'm sure you all know, anyone who is killed by a vampire will turn into one as well and an autopsy on a newborn Vamp is still considered manslaughter. We need to get in there and find out what happened so that those people can be put to rest before they become restless spirits on top of it all.

"Any questions?"

Nobody spoke up, so Marc pointed towards the door. "Directions are already uploaded into your navigation systems. Ty, you've got lead on this one. I'm going to be staying behind to run information between you guys and the police, so make sure that you keep your radios on. Got it?"

They all agreed and headed towards the door. Once again, Jen had to ride with J.J. because she still didn't have a truck of her own. As she fastened her seat belt, she made a mental note to ask David when she would receive her own wheels.

They were stopped almost a quarter mile away from the neighborhood that had been attacked. Yellow police tape stretched across the road with cruisers parked nose to nose just beyond the tape, barring access to the street. Officers, medical crews, and fire response units were parked just outside the barricade, waiting for the all clear to go in and do their jobs.

There were other people milling around as well, onlookers from the surrounding neighborhoods who had come out to see the excitement. Still more people were being led out of the restricted zone, crying families huddled together and led by the emergency crews as they were brought to safety.

Ty had the team park out of the way of the emergency crews and led them on foot up to the barricade. There, he hailed one of the officers. "We're with New World. I believe you're expecting us." He held up his identification for the officer to see.

After a quick glance at his card, the officer lifted the yellow tape and motioned them through. "It's a mess in here," he explained. "Eleven houses attacked and I don't even know how many bodies there are back there."

"Eleven? You found more?"

The officer nodded. "Yeah, but that's the last of it, I'm sure. All of the other families in the area have been evacuated already. Now, we're just working on the houses closer out to the barricade, just to be safe."

The officer stopped and pointed further up

the street. "Just keep going that way, you can't miss it." He turned and headed back to his post at the barricade.

"Okay, I guess we're on our own from here," Ty said as he looked around at the team. "Let's see what we can find."

They walked up the street past vacated houses and silent cars. As the sun slowly crept over the horizon, the street was bathed in a soft yellow glow as the light filtered through the clouds. Most of the houses they passed were neat and tidy, giving no indication of the chaos that had been wreaked further down the street.

Soon, the iron scent of blood filled the air and the team knew they were close. Somehow, the houses in that section of street seemed to be darker, as though the houses themselves had been imbued with the sinister essence of the massacre that had occurred.

The team walked into the first house where a confirmed killing had taken place. At first, nothing seemed to be amiss. Inside the front door, a set of stairs led down on the left, a hallway stretched out to the right, and an archway opened to a large open space before them.

As soon as they crossed the threshold under the archway and into a brightly-lit living room, however, that all changed. Everyone stopped just inside the room to look at the single, severed arm that lay in a pool of blood in the center of the room.

A trail of blood led further into the house and the team followed it into the kitchen, where they found the rest of the body. An elderly man, in his early seventies by Jen's estimation, was slumped against the far wall, as though he had been trying to get to the back door and almost made it before whatever had been after him had finished the task of ending his life. He still wore a pair of khaki pants, now stained with blood, and the denim shirt had been ripped at the shoulder where his arm was removed. Half of his head had been caved in and a single tooth lay on the floor next to him, apparently knocked free in the brutal attack.

Wreckage of the kitchen table lay scattered across the room and a block of knives had been overturned. Knives were scattered everywhere and even a toaster was left to soak in the slowly cooling blood.

After the team had a moment to recover from the grisly sight, they spread out to search the rest of the house. Jen fought down a wave of nausea that threatened to explode as she turned to assist in the search. The first room she went into was a bedroom, the blankets and sheets rumpled as though the man in the kitchen had been in bed when the intruder arrived. A pair of brown corduroy slippers sat waiting next to the bed, partially obscured by the tangle of sheets and blankets. In the far wall, a large, gaping hole stretched from the floor to almost the ceiling. "Hey guys, you might want to see this," she called out.

The rest of the group came in to see what she was talking about and stared in awe at the hole in the wall. Through it, there was a direct line to the next house, with another, identical hole ripped into it as though some juggernaut had simply moved from one house to the next.

"How could anyone have not heard that happen?" she wondered out loud. "It couldn't have been quiet."

Curious but not overly alarmed, the group went out through the hole and across the yard to the next house. There, they found the doorway inside the house had been broken, as though something very wide had passed through it.

There were more bodies inside that house as well, all of them missing pieces and blood trails leading everywhere. After only a couple of minutes of searching, however, Mike ran for the nearest exit.

Jen followed him out, partially because she could use some air as well, and partly to make sure that Mike was okay. He was squatted down on the grass outside, elbows on his knees and taking deep breaths, trying not to retch.

"Did you see that?" he asked her when he came back up to breathe. "It looked like something took a bite out of one of them."

"Yeah, I saw that too." She had to agree with Mike's assessment, one of the chunks that had been ripped out of the woman's body did indeed look as though it had been bitten off rather than just torn. "Are you going to be okay? You can wait out here if you need to."

"No, I'm fine now," he answered as he stood back up. "It was just a bit of a shock, that's all."

She walked with him back into the house,

where they caught back up with the rest of the group. Everyone seemed to be a little green over the carnage but nobody else needed to head out for more air.

Of the eleven houses that they searched, all of them showed similar holes and broken doorways as the first couple had. Furniture lay in pieces in virtually every room of every house but, in houses that had them, basements seemed oddly undisturbed. The group was able to track how the attackers had gotten from one house to the next quite easily by following the holes in the walls between them. Finally, Ty called back to the office. "Marc, are you still talking with the police?"

"Yes. Have you found something?"

"We're still looking, but could you ask them to check the evacuees and see if anyone heard anything last night? Every house we've been to had at least one hole smashed in an exterior wall, so someone had to have heard something."

"Okay, I'll check. If you find anything else, let me know."

"Will do." He turned back to the rest of the team. "Well, I think we can all agree that none of these are coming back as vampires, so that's at least a start. Anybody else have any observations?"

"Might be Weres," J.J. offered. "Could have been one of their hunting parties came through here."

"Weres wouldn't have smashed holes in the walls like this," Mike disagreed. "Whatever this was, it's more violent than a Were. Besides, the moon wasn't full last night and only a few of the bodies seem to have been chewed on. Weres would have eaten a lot more."

"Hey, look at this," Jen called their attention to one of the bodies. "This one looks like it was cut with a blade of some sort."

The rest of them gathered around the body to see what she was talking about. "Yeah, it does," Ty agreed. "Had to have been a big damn knife to do that much damage, though."

"Knife, or sword?" Mike asked.

"What?" Ty asked.

"Well, those knights from the other day, they had swords, didn't they? And they were big enough that they would be able to smash through the walls like this."

Ty nodded. "You've got a point, but there's still no way to be sure. It seems pretty unlikely that the black knights would have been able to tear through this area like that and have nobody notice."

They continued their investigation. It looked as though some of the victims had attempted to fight back against the intruders because recently fired guns, knives, and even a few baseball bats and other bludgeoning weapons were scattered throughout the row of damaged houses. Soon, Marc called back to relay that nobody from the surrounding houses had heard anything that could have been the walls being broken.

"What about gunfire? Were there any reports of shots fired in this area last night?" Ty asked.

"Hang on a sec, let me find out." After a brief pause, Marc came back on the radio. "Yes, there was one report of someone hearing gunfire last night. But before anyone went out to investigate, a call came in about the body discovery."

"Think you can find out what time that call came in? There're defensive weapons all over the place out here, so it's pretty likely that whenever that report came in, that's when they were under attack."

"Makes sense," Marc agreed, "and that's more than what we had to go on before. Have you found anything else?"

"Just a bunch of carnage. To be honest, I don't think that there are enough transport rigs outside the perimeter to carry all the bodies out."

"Have you been keeping count?"

With a heavy sigh, Ty said, "Yes. There are forty-three bodies so far, and we aren't even sure that's all of them."

Marc whistled over the radio. "That's a lot more than I'd expected. How's the team holding up?"

"About as well as can be expected. I'll let you know when we know more."

They went back through all of the houses, looking for anything that might have gone un-noticed at the first pass. Ty pulled out his camera for the second walkthrough and started to take photographs of the different damaged spots on the walls, the scattered weapons, the broken furniture, and the wounds on each of the bodies.

J.J. did make an unusual discovery at one house as they passed through. "Hey, there are people outside!"

Everyone went out to see who was there, but their hopes of finding survivors faded quickly, as they discovered that the people outside were just as dead as the people inside had been. These bodies were actually in worse shape than the previous ones had been, they looked as though they had been pummeled by a very large meat tenderizer. One of them had been beaten so badly that his head hung loosely from his shoulders with only a few scraps of tendon keeping it from falling off completely.

Jen stopped cold at the sight, knowing that she had seen that before. For a brief moment, she was standing in a pile of bodies during the Festival of Souls, watching one of the black knights' hideous mounts try to rip the head off of one of its victims.

"I knew they weren't gone," she said as she looked down at the corpse. "I just knew it."

They looked around the area and, as she had suspected, quickly discovered large cloven hoof prints, sunk deep into the soil as though pressed down with tremendous weight. "Are you satisfied now?" Jen looked at her teammates.

Mike nodded. "Looks like it's not over yet after all."

Once they finished with their second pass through the punctured houses, the team headed back up the road to where the police still waited. They waved down the same officer that had let them through the barrier on the way in and told him that it would be safe to send the medical examiners in to pick up the bodies. "We're certain that this wasn't a vampire attack, so there shouldn't be any legal problem with getting them out of there and taken care of."

Nobody was surprised that there hadn't been any reports of mounted horsemen in the area, so once the medical examiner's people started to gather the bodies and the New World team had a chance to rest for a few minutes, they were allowed to move their vehicles into the restricted area so that they could start following the tracks that they had found and perhaps find out where the black knights had gone.

They started at the house where they had first found the hoof prints, from where it was fairly short work to find more tracks. They walked through the yards on foot, taking pictures of every hoof print they found and marking their personal GPS units so that they could find the tracks again, if need be.

For over an hour, they followed the prints as the tracks became more and more scarce. When they arrived at a graveled area, they knew that the chances of finding the tracks again were slim. Finally, they had to admit that the knights had escaped them again. With nothing more they could do at that point, they packed up their gear and headed back to the office to file their reports.

Shortly after arriving at the office, Jen discovered that she had missed a call from Sahara. "Hey, I figured I should remind you about Collin's birthday party tomorrow. It's at two, so whenever you want to be here is cool." Jen swore as she listened to the message. With all that had been going on, she had completely forgotten about Collin's first birthday party.

Quickly, she headed for her locker to change out of her gear, thankful that she had gotten into the habit of keeping a change of clothes in her locker for just such an emergency. "I'll send my reports in by tonight, I promise," she called over to Marc as she ran for the elevator, "but something's come up, and I have to go!"

"Do you need backup?" he called after her as she waited for the elevator doors to open.

"Maybe," she answered as she stepped inside. "I'll call if I need help." As the doors closed, she wracked her brain, trying to think of what a one-year-old would want for his presents.

She climbed into her Jeep and headed out for the closest toy store she could think of, only breaking a couple of speed limits on the way there. She pulled up into the parking lot in front of The Toybox, a popular kids' store, and all but ran for the doors.

Inside, the store was brightly lit and garishly colored. Flashing lights, bells, and whistles called for attention from every direction.

Jen stopped just inside the door, searching for where to start first. As she scanned the store, a young man wearing a nametag that read Kevin approached her. "Can I help you find something?"

She reached out and took him by the arm. "Yes. I have a birthday party and no presents. This needs to be fixed."

He laughed. "Okay, no problem. How old is the..." he looked over at her questioningly. "Boy?"

"He's one," she responded. "And I forgot."

Kevin led her off to a corner of the store where all of the shelves were stuffed to overflowing with toys of all shapes, sizes, and colors. "What types of things does he like?"

Jen shrugged and let go of his arm. "I don't know, kid stuff I guess." She looked at the shelves, feeling almost as lost in the selection of toddler toys as she had felt upon walking into the store. "I think I'm gonna need a basket."

Kevin offered to go get one for her. While he was gone, she pulled down a toy that looked sufficiently noisy. It was a plastic train set that advertised a working bell, whistle, and other realistic train noises. She set it on the floor next to her and continued perusing the shelves.

By the time Kevin came back with the cart, she had added an enormous stuffed dog, a package of small toy cars, three floating bath ducks that squirted water, and a toy fishing pole to the pile at her feet. She scooped up all the packages and dumped them into the cart before turning back to the shelves. If the kid was getting a fishing pole, he would need things to fish for, she figured, so she added a package of sea creatures to the basket. She also added a toy barn that came with about a hundred animals, a remote-controlled race car, and a plush monkey that squawked when you squeezed it.

"Some of these toys will be too old for him to immediately enjoy," Kevin explained as he helped her load her cart, "but he will grow into them quickly enough."

"And he has two older brothers, so I'm pretty sure there will be plenty of playing with everything."

Kevin pushed the cart along with her as she shopped, pointing out a handful of other items that Collin might like as well. Everything that he recommended, including the markers that only worked on a special kind of paper and crayons that wiped easily off of walls, she added to the cart. He was the expert, after all. Finally, once she was completely out of room to add more, she headed to the checkout line.

She discovered that the truly hard part was stuffing everything into her truck. Not for the first time, she was glad that the Jeep had plenty of interior room but even then, it was a bit of a squeeze. Once she got it all inside, however, she realized that she had forgotten wrapping paper and ribbon.

Fifteen minutes later, she was on the highway and heading home. All she had left to do was wrap the presents and she was done. "See?" She pointed out to the enormous stuffed dog that was buckled into the passenger seat, "That wasn't so bad after all."

When she got home, she discovered her next challenge. Most of the presents she had purchased were not in nice square or rectangular boxes, so wrapping them wouldn't be as easy as she thought it would be. Even the gifts that were in nice, tidy boxes proved difficult as the wrapping paper tore when she tried to cut it and the boxes changed size so that the sheets of paper she cut turned out to be too small for what she was trying to wrap.

Finally, in frustration, she gave up completely and went off in search of boxes. She pulled out the three largest boxes that she could find around the house, dragged them out to her driveway, and then went over to Troy's car in search of spray paint. "I know you have some," she grumbled as she popped the trunk open. "You have every other damn thing on the planet in here, so where's the paint?"

"It's in the back seat." Jen jumped as Troy spoke up from behind her. He reached in through the open driver door and pulled a plastic bag from the floorboard behind the seat.

Jen took the bag and peered inside. Three cans of paint, one yellow, one blue, and one green, were inside. "Perfect," she took the bag over to the trio of boxes and began to coat them in bright colors.

Once all of the boxes were covered in a thick

coating of paint, she gave the bag of paint cans back to Troy. "How long does that stuff take to dry?" she asked.

A couple hours later, after the paint had set, she dragged the boxes back inside. On the kitchen table, she stuffed each of them with as many toys as she could fit inside before taping the flaps closed and, using a large quantity of tape on each, wrapped yards of ribbons around each of them. She emptied the bag of bows she had bought, separated it into three piles, and taped one pile onto each of the boxes.

The handful of things that wouldn't fit into the boxes were quickly shoved into a gift bag, which she stapled closed to secure. "See? No problem at all."

# Chapter 8

Early the next morning, Jen was woken by a crashing sound in the living room. "What the hell did those idiots break?" she wondered aloud as she crawled out of bed and headed out of her room. It wouldn't be the first time that Troy or Patrick had gotten up in the middle of the night and either tripped over something or dropped something. Seriously, at the rate they were going, she was lucky to have much left. She pulled her taser out of her drawer, swearing that, after tonight, they would pay a little more attention to what they were doing. She was having a hard enough time sleeping; she didn't need to have them waking her up like this.

When she stepped out of her room, however, she knew that something was wrong. Reddish orange flashes of color were splayed across her living room, and it took her a moment to realize that the flashes of color were tongues of flame. "Why is my carpet on fire?" she asked as she looked around the room. The taser wouldn't do much against that, she was certain.

"Get down!" Patrick called out. The front window was broken and Patrick and Troy were both on the floor. Troy was halfway to the front door when something flew in through the already-broken window. More fire exploded across her living room and finally Jen recognized what was happening.

She leapt out of the way of the fire and darted for the kitchen, looking for something to smother the blaze. Vaguely, she remembered seeing her mother using baking soda to put out a kitchen fire and she hoped it worked as well on the carpet as it did on the stove. She grabbed the box out of the fridge and headed back to the living room.

As she shook a generous amount of the powder onto the fire, another bottle came in through the window. Unlike all the previous ones, that one didn't explode and Patrick had the presence of mind to yank the burning piece of cloth from the bottle before it ignited, too.

The howl of a motor outside, combined with the squeal of tires, let them know that who-ever had just tried to set Jen's house ablaze was making his escape. Closest to the door, Troy ran outside but when he came back in a few moments later, all he carried was a fire extin-guisher.

He shook his head when he noticed Jen's questioning look. "They're already gone."

Between the baking soda and the fire extin-guisher they were able to put out the last of the flames. Jen stood in the middle of her destroyed living room and looked around at the damage. Her carpet was gone; most of the cheap ma-terial had melted as soon as the first firebomb had touched down. Her couch had received a lot of damage; parts of it had holes burned into it and the entire front panel had been burned completely through. She wasn't entirely certain how her coffee table had gotten broken but it was on its side and one of the legs was missing completely. Shards of glass covered her floor and a cold wind blew in through the hole in her wall where the window had been.

Troy's recliner had taken some damage as well and Jen knew that it would have to be reupholstered, at the very least. At some point, he had shoved his duffel bag against the far wall so it sat unscathed next to Patrick's suitcases. Probably a good thing the bag had been out of range of the fire, she realized. There was no way of knowing how many explosives or otherwise combustible things were in that bag.

Slowly, Jen walked back to her bedroom to get her phone. "Hello, police? I need an officer to stop by, someone just torched my house."

Police cruisers, a pair of fire trucks, and an ambulance showed up in quick succession. Jen explained about what had happened and Patrick brought out the bottle of liquid that hadn't exploded. After one sniff, the officer grimaced. "No wonder it burned so quickly, this smells like kerosene."

Since the fire was already out, there was no need for the fire trucks to be there so they were sent off almost immediately. Nobody had been seriously injured, so after checking the three of them to make sure they weren't suffering from smoke inhalation, the ambulance left also. "Of course we weren't inhaling smoke," Jen explained, "the window was open."

The police spent more time talking with Troy than any of the others; mostly because he was the only one to have gone outside and had at least a rudimentary description of the vehicle the arsonist had been in. While he was giving his statement, Jen and Patrick went back into the house to start cleaning up the mess.

Patrick pulled out his phone and called Nacho, asking him to bring over some plywood. "That'll at least help for now. Once I can get another window to put in, I'll get the rest of the wall fixed."

They pulled up the carpet, there wasn't enough left of it to save. A lot of the glass that had been blown out of the window had actually melted into the carpet, so that made some of the cleanup easier. The house still stank of fire and kerosene, not to mention whatever chemical had been in the fire extinguisher that Troy used. No matter what it said on the canister;

Jen didn't entirely believe that it had contained a standard mixture of repellant. Troy wasn't capable of leaving well enough alone, not even a simple fire extinguisher.

After the police, media, and all of the neighborhood gawkers had left and as much of the mess in the living room had been cleaned up as they could manage, Jen hauled the last of the debris to the trash bin and checked the time. It was after ten by then, so even on a Saturday most businesses should be open. She walked out to the kitchen and poured herself a cup of coffee before picking up the phone book from the top of the fridge. She sat at the kitchen table, sipping at her coffee and flipping through the yellow pages.

Finding the number she wanted, she flipped open her phone and dialed. "Hello, McKenzie Realty? I need a new house." It was the same realtor she had used when she bought her current house. Her last experience had been good so she saw no reason to go with a different realtor.

Troy walked in as she spoke to a realtor, and poured himself some more coffee. He leaned against the counter and listened to her half of the conversation. When Jen hung up a few minutes later, he poured more coffee into her cup. "You don't have to do that, you know. It can be fixed."

"I know. Patrick's good, and I'm sure you have some nifty new ideas for upgrades, too. But honestly, I've been thinking that the house is too small for all three of us, and this was just the last straw."

"Are you sure this is what you want?"

Jen sighed. "Right now, yeah. I want a place that hasn't been set on fire. We can fix the living room and then I can sell this place or something. Maybe keep it as a rental, I really don't know. Either way, I still need a bigger house." What she didn't say was that she wanted a new house where her location wasn't already known to someone who had tried to burn her in her sleep. Even without voicing her true feelings, it was apparent that Troy understood her deeper meaning.

Troy nodded and looked at the pile of birthday gifts for Collin that still sat on the table where Jen had left them after wrapping them.

"I guess it's a good thing that you didn't bring these out already."

"Yeah, no kidding." She looked at her watch. "I think I'm going to head over to Sahara's early. Maybe I can help her set up for the party or something."

Troy nodded. "Let her know we'll be there pretty soon. I told Patrick I'd help him pick up a few things on the way."

"Okay." She headed back to the bedroom to grab her coat. The weather had only gotten worse during the morning and an icy rain had begun to fall. Once she had her coat on and grabbed her keys, she went back out to the kitchen, stacked the boxes so that she could carry them all, and headed out for her truck. "I guess there's not much point in locking up, is there?" She looked over at Patrick as she walked through the door.

On the way to Sahara's house, she called the New World Response office. When David answered, she explained about the fire at her house. "I won't be coming in for workout today like I had planned to."

David was sympathetic. "No problem. If you

can make it in tomorrow, that's fine, but if not, don't worry about it. I can sign off on your card for this week."

"Thanks. I'll see what I can do about tomorrow." She pulled up in front of Sahara's house as she hung up the phone. After wrestling the packages out of the truck, she staggered up to the front door and kicked it until it opened.

"Whoa, here, let me help you with those," Joel's voice floated around the boxes as he pulled the top two from the stack she held. "You're here early."

"Yeah, it's been a morning," Jen explained as she followed him inside. "Where do these go?"

He led her into the living room where a small pile of gifts had already accumulated. They added her presents to the stack and Joel escorted her into the kitchen where Sahara was busily putting the finishing touches on Collin's birthday cake, humming along to the radio as she decorated.

"You're early," Sahara commented when she looked up to discover Jen, who was busily pouring herself a cup of coffee. "And you look like hell. Rough morning?"

"I've decided to move," she explained as she leaned against the counter to take a drink.

Sahara blinked at her. "What brought that about?"

Jen shrugged. "There was a fire in my living room this morning and I just got fed up with it all. Besides, there are three of us there right now, and even if one of the guys leaves, the house is still too small."

Sahara set down the spatula and looked at her with wide eyes. "Fire? What happened?"

Jen explained about the drive-by arson. "Everyone's okay," she reassured her friend. "And the presents are fine."

"Oh, forget the presents," Sahara shushed her. "I'm just glad you guys are all right."

"No, don't forget the presents," Jen protested. "You have no idea how much effort I spent on those." She took another drink of her coffee and smiled at her friend. "Have you been to The Toybox lately? It's a nightmare."

Sahara put Jen to work hanging up streamers and blowing up balloons. "The kids are out with my mom so we've got some time to finish getting ready. Since you're here early, I'm going to assume it's because you don't mind helping set up," she explained.

Jen raised her hands in submission and accepted the box of decorations. "Kinda figured you could use a hand. That's why I'm here."

By the time the boys got home from their grandmother's house, most of the living room was covered in crepe paper and balloons. They bombed in through the front door and stopped to look around the room in amazement. "Whoa," Don exclaimed. "That's a lot of decorations!"

Jen grinned down at them. "Yep, and it's almost time for all the guests to show up, too." She ushered the two older boys off towards their rooms. "Go get changed so you can be ready for the party, okay?"

When the guests started to show up, everyone had changed into clean clothes and Nicholas had even managed to clean the smudge of colored chalk off his cheeks. Soon the party was in full swing. Some of the kids' friends from the neighborhood showed up and they proceeded to run at full speed through the house, dodging between the adults as they played balloon volleyball. A lot of Sahara and Joel's friends came as well, bearing colorful boxes and bags full of gifts.

A couple of the guests who showed up were friends that Jen hadn't seen in a long time. Cathy Hartley was a striking woman who stood almost an inch taller than Jen in her heels, with sleek, vibrant red hair and a generous smile. She carried her youngest child, Amy, an adorable little girl with strawberry-blond curls. As soon as they were in the door, Amy struggled to be let down so that she could run off with the rest of the kids.

Angie showed up as well, and to everyone's surprise, Eric came with her. The poltergeist floated in through the door behind her, being unusually quiet. "We had a long talk about it," Angie explained when Jen came over to talk with her, "and he promised to behave while he's here."

"But why is he here? I thought he was bound to his house."

Angie nodded. "But apparently possession goes a bit further than that. Since I own the house, apparently I own him, too. That means he can go out where I go but I have to decide to let him come."

Jen burst out laughing. "That sucks for him, doesn't it?"

Angie shrugged, smirking. "I told him that if he behaved while we were here, we'd go to a strip bar later."

When Troy and Patrick arrived, they brought surprise guests with them as well. A young man with the same slender build, dark hair and dark eyes as Jen, walked through the door behind Patrick.

"Todd!" Jen shrieked as she ran over to hug him. "I didn't know you were coming!"

"Like I could miss this," he laughed as he hugged her back. "We all got the reminder, you know."

Just behind Todd was a woman who was only a couple years older than Patrick. She had rich mahogany curls, just a hint of perfectly applied makeup, and was very stylishly dressed. She carried a few silver gift bags. Jaime was the eldest of her siblings and Jen had always felt a bit shadowed in her presence. She was the one who had inherited all of the style genes and now worked in the advertising department for Lady Bella, her favorite clothing company. "Just because you can't keep your dates straight you always seem to think that we can't, either." She stepped around Todd to give Jen a hug. "It's been too long, though." Looking between perfectly polished Jaime and scruffy Jen, most people had difficulty believing that the two were sisters.

Mary, their youngest sister, was quick to dart in the door behind her. "Brr," she shivered, "it's pretty cold out there." She was bundled up in a thick jacket and a knit cap that had puff balls that dangled down over her ears. "Why is it so much colder here than it is at home?" She pulled off the mittens and cap once she was safely inside, revealing a mess of tight brown curls that fell to just below her ears.

Troy followed the group in, smirking at Jen as he walked past her. "Like I said, I had to help Patrick pick up a few things." He ducked as Jen swatted him and snickered towards the kitchen. Jen could see him eyeing Jaime as he walked past her, as most men did. Jen couldn't really blame him for looking; her sister was gorgeous.

Jen enjoyed visiting with her siblings while the kids tore through the house. They sat in the living room watching balloons and streamers fly and catching up on what each of them had been up to.

Todd was still working with Viceroy, the magical research facility out on the east coast. "Everyone back at the office loved your team's reports on the nullifying enchantment," he explained to Jen. A little while ago, Todd had helped Jen out of a tight spot by supplying her with one of his new, barely tested spells. In return, Jen had agreed to send in some field study reports to show that the spell worked as he had intended. "Because of the positive review, we're going to look into production for the military pretty soon."

"That's awesome," she grinned at him. "With all the crap that's going on lately, I'm sure they could use it, too."

He grinned back at her. "Where's yours? I've

had a couple people ask about the strange title you gave it so I wanted to borrow it and bring it back to show them."

"I don't have it any more. It got broken while we were using it."

It was Todd's turn to look surprised. "How did you break it? That was, technically speaking, a magical implement. It shouldn't have broken that easily."

Jen shook her head. "Not now. I'll tell you all about what happened but this isn't a good place for it." She wasn't about to explain in front of this large group of people that she had broken the Clue-by-Four while dismantling a gateway to hell. To change the topic, she turned to her sisters. "What have you guys been up to?"

Jaime spoke up first. "I got the promotion I was aiming for, so that's my big news. I'm now the overseer for the southwest division."

"Awesome," Jen congratulated her sister. "I'm sure you've already started the next step in your takeover." When Jaime had first announced that she had gotten a sales position with Lady Bella, there had been a lot of teasing about how long it would take for Jaime to take over the company. So far it had been just over four years and she was well on her way to doing precisely that.

Mary was doing well also. She was on her way to becoming a qualified veterinarian and had already signed up for an internship with a clinic near her school. "I start in two weeks and I'm really nervous about it."

"You're going to do fine," they all reassured her.

When the time came to open the gifts, Jaime handed over the silver bags she had brought. "These are from our new Baby Bling line, and they haven't even hit the stores yet." Inside, there were about a dozen outfits ranging in size from one year old to eighteen months. "Just because he's small, that doesn't mean he can't be stylish" she quipped.

Mary had brought presents as well but as she handed out the assortment of bags, she looked a bit sheepish. "I couldn't remember whose birthday it was, so I brought stuff for all of you." She handed over a box each to Collin, Nicholas, Don, and even a pair of boxes to Sahara and Joel. "I figured that this way, I had everyone covered and I've never seen anyone turn down an extra present."

Todd admitted that he hadn't brought any gifts. "I actually had some, I can send them once I get home but they're still sitting in my living room, right where I left them."

Sahara tried to tell him that it was okay because Collin had already gotten more than enough but he insisted that he had a couple of surprises left under his sleeve. "I'm sure we can come up with something."

Jen sat back, knowing what was about to happen. By the look in her brother's eyes, she knew that he hadn't forgotten a thing and he knew exactly what he was doing. He stepped into the middle of the room and, with a wave of his arm, a cloud of smoke appeared around him. When the smoke dissipated, he was dressed in a deep purple robe that was covered in shimmering, silvery stars. He grinned down at the kids.

Nicholas looked over at Jen, his eyes huge. "You didn't tell us your brother was a wizard!"

As the kids clapped and cheered, Todd performed a handful of illusions, causing sparkling designs in the air, making the kids fly across the ceiling and even turning an empty, discarded piece of wrapping paper into a toy plane for the birthday boy.

When he was finished, he sank back into his seat and let the illusion of wizard robes fade until he was back in his street clothes. "I haven't done a show like that since my second year at the academy," he whispered over to Jen.

"It was fantastic," she whispered back. "I'm not sure who had more fun with that, the kids or the parents!"

Once all of the presents had been opened, Joel brought out a stack of pizzas, followed by Troy, who had been roped into carrying the paper plates. Everyone dove into the feast and soon there was almost no pizza left.

While they were all eating, Sahara brought Jen into the kitchen to help her with the cake. "I wasn't supposed to tell you that they were coming," she explained. "Patrick said that he wanted it to be a surprise for you, too."

"Well, that it was," Jen agreed. "I think they were about the last thing I was expecting to-day."

After the cake was served, Jen stayed around

for a little while to help clean up the mess. Troy and Patrick took Todd, Jaime, and Mary to their hotel so that they could get settled in and by the time she got back home that night, Troy was already there.

"Patrick's still at the hotel," he explained when Jen walked in. "It looked like a family thing, so I figured it'd be better to leave them to it."

Jen nodded and headed to the kitchen to fire up a pot of coffee. While it was brewing, she looked over her ruined living room. Although most of the mess had been cleaned up, the sight still saddened her. "The realtor said she had a couple places open so I'm going to go down to their office tomorrow and get the list. Maybe there'll be something open now that'll work for us."

Troy walked over to stand next to her, surveying the room from her vantage point. "You still don't have to do that, you know. Once we get this fixed up, it'll be good as new." He turned to look at her. "And Patrick and I were talking earlier, too. He said that it wouldn't be any trouble for the two of us to go get a rental but the main reason he wanted to stay with you was because of all the crap that's been going on lately. He's worried about you, and honestly, I am too."

"I know, and I didn't want to worry any of you. That was the main reason I hadn't wanted to get my family involved. They were all off doing their own thing and they were safe where they were." She looked over at Troy. "But now they're all here and I don't know what's going to happen. There's already someone out there trying to kill me and who knows what they'll do if they find out I have family in the area."

"Is that why you're not at the hotel with them?"

She nodded. "I don't want to put any of them in danger. After what they tried to do here, I don't want someone to set their hotel on fire just because I was spotted there." She sighed and turned back into the kitchen to pour some coffee. From the smell, the pot was done making its magic. "At least my parents are still off on their vacation, so they should be all right."

"I'll go get another house and it'll be fine," she said after returning with a fresh cup.

"There'll be room for the both of you, so even if you have to share a bedroom, at least neither of you will have to sleep on the couch or in a recliner in the living room.

"I want another bathroom, too, because nobody should have to go into the bathroom after either of you." She glared at her friend in mock anger. "Particularly after you have had tacos."

Troy laughed at that and poured a cup of coffee for himself as well. "Okay, you have your mind made up. Just promise me that you'll take me with you when you head out to look. Like you said, there's still someone out there that's after you, so if that's all I can do to keep you safe, so be it."

Jen sighed. "Fine. But I want you to remember that it's my decision what house I get, not yours. Understood?"

"Got it."

He probably would have added more, but Jen's phone rang. She stepped away to answer it when she recognized the office number. "What's up?"

"We've got news," David sounded pleased. "The police have been able to identify the person that attacked you in the hospital. They ran the prints off the bottle that survived your house and the prints match up to a person that looks a lot like the person in the surveillance videos. He even has a car similar to the one that Troy said he saw outside your house this morning."

"They got the guy? That's awesome!" Jen looked over at Troy and shot him a thumbs-up. With everything that had happened, she had almost forgotten about the attack in the hospital during the last lunar event, even though it had only been a handful of days since it had happened. Finding out that it had been the same man at her house with the firebombs that morning was unexpected. She should have known better, though. Anyone with enough determination to attack her in the lunar wing of the hospital wouldn't be so easily dissuaded from trying again.

"Not quite," David explained. "They know who he is but they haven't actually found him. It appears as though he hasn't been home in a while and he hasn't been going to work, either."

"Damn." Jen's face fell at the news. "I was hoping that this was over."

"Not quite, but I just wanted to let you know that there has been some progress."

"Thanks, I appreciate that," she responded before hanging up. Once she was off the phone, she explained the update to Troy. "I guess that means they're still looking for him."

"That's something, though," he said as he offered her coffee cup over to her. "At least they're looking and not just leaving it in a report on someone's desk."

Jen nodded and headed out of the kitchen. "Speaking of progress, I think the TV survived the fire." She walked out to the living room and picked up the set, dragging cords behind her as she brought it into the kitchen. "The news should be on soon," she explained as she turned it on.

There wasn't a whole lot of surprising information in the news. There were a handful of feel-good stories, not really what Jen considered news but interesting to watch nevertheless. Politicians were still spouting out their garbage but Jen had decided long ago not to trust what any of them said, especially when there was an election coming up.

A report on another theft in town caught her attention. This time, a private home was broken into and a relic known as the Tiara of Venus was stolen. "The owner of the Tiara didn't immediately realize that the item had been stolen," the reporter explained, "because the Tiara wasn't out on display. He reported the theft after getting into his safe and discovering it was missing."

"That seems awfully strange," Jen mused as she watched the report. "We don't normally get a lot of high-end thefts here. Most of the thefts we get are nickel and dime robberies."

"You think there's a connection?" Troy asked her.

Jen shrugged. "Maybe. But this is the third theft this month, nobody's seen anything, nobody's gotten any leads from them, and none of the missing stuff has turned up." She looked over at her friend. "Granting that the first theft was a jewelry store and the second, that was a museum, wasn't it?" When Troy nodded, she put her elbow on the table and her chin in her hand to think. "They never said what was missing from the museum but the first one was jewelry and a tiara's kind of like jewelry, isn't it? So maybe there's a connection there."

"You think there's a jewel thief in the area?" Troy snickered. "Come on, those only happen in detective stories."

Jen was the top story of the night again, as the bombing of her house was apparently the most exciting thing that had happened that day. There was footage of her house, both from early that morning while the fire crews had still been there as well as more that had apparently been shot while she was gone because it was daylight and her truck wasn't there.

"Great," she muttered as she saw herself on the report. "Just what I needed." In case there was anyone else out there with a serious grudge against her, finding out where she lived had just become a lot easier. Thankfully, she was already planning on rectifying that particular problem.

During the story, they recapped the attempted murder at the hospital and showed the surveillance footage of the suspect. They also placed a picture that looked like an employee identification photo, on the screen. "The suspect has been identified as Timothy Jergens, a local teenager. He was reported missing by his parents over a week ago, after what they referred to as 'unusual' behavior. At this point, Jergens is suspected of acting under the influence of a controlled substance, possibly cocaine. Anybody who sees him is encouraged to contact the police, but do not approach him, as he is considered to be armed and extremely dangerous."

"Why can't they find this kid?" Jen asked as she turned the set off. "He can't be that hard to find, so what's taking so long?"

Troy tried to reassure her, but she wouldn't listen. "I'm going to get a bath and go to bed. If anyone else wants to burn the house down tonight, eat them."

Lying in bed that night, Jen tossed and turned, trying to get comfortable so that she could sleep. Even though she hadn't wanted to admit it, she was scared. She still didn't know why she had someone trying to kill her and, as she had told Troy, she was worried about her family. With them in town, they were in very real danger and she doubted that any of them even knew it.

She was also worried about buying a new house. She knew that she needed a bigger place and she would be more comfortable somewhere that hadn't been so thoroughly covered in the news but the truth was, she hated moving. Not that it would be hard, as she didn't own much, but just the idea of picking up and leaving one place and starting over somewhere new where she didn't know any of the neighbors or the people at the corner grocery mart.

Her phone rang as she turned over again, and she swore. When she picked up the phone, she didn't recognize the number and groaned, hoping it wasn't the media. She had kept her number unlisted on purpose. "Yeah?"

"Is this Jen Rice?"

"Depends on whether you have a really good reason for calling at one in the morning," she snarled into the phone.

"I do apologize but I have a problem and I was told that you were probably the only person that might be able to help."

"Look, it's late and I'm trying to sleep. What do you want?"

"I was told to be honest with you, so I intend to be as honest as I can be. That having been said, I should let you know that I am the one that's been all over the news lately."

Jen sat up in bed. "You're the one trying to kill me? What the hell is this, some sort of joke?"

"No, I'm not trying to kill you, that wasn't what I meant. I'm the one that the police are searching for regarding a series of heists as of late."

Jen blinked. "The jewel thief? Why are you calling me? I don't deal in that stuff."

"No, but you have talents in another area of which I have need. You see, I am not doing any of this by my choice but because I have been ordered to do them."

"I don't understand."

"It's my daughter. She has been stolen and if I don't do as I am instructed, she will be destroyed forever. So, you see, I have no choice and I need your help."

"So... what? You want me to find your daughter?"

"Basically, yes, that is the crux of it. I have tried to find her on my own but have been having no success. I am hoping that you would have a better go of it."

"Why me? Shouldn't you have called the police?"

"I did try, but they didn't appear to want to listen. That leaves you as the best option I have left."

"Again, why me? Why do you think I'll be able to help you find her?"

"Because of your success against the demon last month. If anyone can perform the nigh impossible, it would be you." On the other end of the line, she heard him sigh. "Look, I am willing to turn myself in for the thefts and submit to whatever your human courts decree but first I must have my daughter returned to me safely. Only then can I relent."

"Human courts?" she repeated. "What are you?"

"As of this moment, that doesn't matter.

The basic facts remain, so all I need is to know if you are willing to help me."

Jen took a minute to think about it. The caller's cryptic manner of speaking led her to believe that this was an invitation to some sort of a trap but he sounded genuine, whatever he was. She could also believe that, not being human, perhaps that was just the way he spoke. "Fine, I'll see what I can do," she relented, against her own better judgement. She just hoped that she lived long enough to regret it.

"Excellent. I will call you in a few days, once I have arranged a suitable place for us to meet."

"Great. Can I go back to sleep now?"

"Of course. When I call you, I will also have the man who has been attempting on your life. Tit for tat, as it were. Sweet dreams, and all that such. You shall hear from me soon." As soon as he finished speaking, the line went dead, so she assumed that meant he had hung up.

"Great," she muttered as she put the phone down and fell over onto the bed. "What have I gotten into this time?"

# Chapter 9

When Jen rolled out of bed the next morning, she scowled at the alarm. There was no reason for her to have to get up after only a few hours' sleep and she couldn't quite wrap her foggy brain over why the alarm clock had insisted on waking her. She stumbled towards the kitchen and discovered that the coffee had already been started and there was just under a half pot left. Sending up a prayer of thanks to the coffee gods for sending someone to make her morning just a little bit easier, she poured a cup and gathered her thoughts, trying to make her eyes focus.

The phone book still lay open on the counter where she had left it, which reminded her why she had needed to be awake. "Oh yeah," she nodded as she took another drink of her coffee. "I'm supposed to get the list today."

Strange sounds from outside caught her attention and she wandered towards the window to see what was going on. The living room was strangely dim for that time of morning and it took her a second to remember that the window was boarded over. Cautiously, she opened her front door to have a peek outside, hoping that whatever was making the noise wouldn't attack her until she had at least been able to get dressed.

To her surprise, she found Nacho and Jose in her front yard, hauling an enormous cardboard box up to the side of her house. Their truck was parked behind her Jeep and Paco stood in the back of the truck, pulling out tools. When Nacho and Jose reached the front wall of her house, they set the box on the ground and leaned it against her front wall, just past where the plywood that Patrick had put up ended.

When Jose looked up and saw Jen, he smiled and waved. "Patrick wanted us to bring over a new window for you." Leaving the box for

Nacho to open, he jogged over to Jen. "He's tied up with the electrical team today, so he figured we'd have enough time to get the new window in place by the time he was done."

She nodded and took another sip of her coffee. "Well, if you need anything, I'll be inside."

She closed the door and walked across her living room, surprised that Troy was still asleep, with all the noise that the guys were making outside. Shrugging it away, she poured herself another cup of motivation and headed for the shower.

By the time she finished in the bathroom and got dressed, Troy was already awake and halfway through his own breakfast. "I thought you wanted to head out this morning," he looked up from his toast as she walked into the room.

"I am," she answered as she poured another cup of coffee. "But I wanted to get a shower first, don't you?" She leaned over and sniffed the hybrid. "You smell kind of ripe, there."

He lifted and arm and sniffed as well. Making a face, he flinched. "Yep, definitely time for a flea dip." He swallowed the last of his food and headed off to get cleaned up.

As soon as he was finished getting ready, they headed out to her truck. Before they left, however, Jen stopped by to talk to Paco, Nacho, and Jose. "I'm going to leave the door unlocked," she explained, "so if you guys need anything, you can get inside. Just don't make too much of a mess, okay?"

They agreed, so she and Troy headed out. Their first stop was at the realty agent's office, where they appreciated the complimentary coffee service while waiting for the agent to finish her phone call. After she hung up, she looked up at them and smiled. "Hi, how can I help you?"

Deborah McKenzie was a stout woman, maybe forty-five years old, with slightly graying hair and reading glasses that hung on a beaded chain around her neck. She had a pleasant smile and had an air of competence about her without all the fuss that would normally be found in a larger place.

Jen stood up and walked over to the woman. "I'm Jen Rice, we spoke on the phone earlier."

"Ah, yes, I remember. You can call me Deborah." She rifled through some papers on her desk. "You had said you were looking for a house, correct?"

"Yes, that's right." Jen sat in one of the chairs that waited in front of the desk. "The neighborhood that I live in now has gotten a little bit too much attention lately and I want a bit more privacy."

Deborah nodded, smiling knowingly at Jen and Troy. "I can understand that, privacy can be pretty important." She picked up a small stack of papers and offered them to Jen. "I have a listing of houses in the area. You hadn't mentioned what your price range was, so I have them in order from the least expensive to the more high-end residences."

Jen took the list and flipped through it as Deborah continued. "You can go and look at each of the houses and, if you find something you like, you can call me and I'll come down with the keys. I don't have anything planned for today, so I'll be available until about five thirty or so."

"Okay, that should work," Jen commented absently, barely listening as she looked at the photos in the packet. There were over a dozen houses and when she looked at the prices listed for the ones towards the back, she almost choked. Apparently housing prices had gone up since she had bought her last house. "I'll give you a call if I find anything I'm interested in looking at."

She gathered up Troy and they headed out in search of a new place to live. While they drove, he took the list and scanned through it, whistling under his breath as he saw some of the prices. "Are you sure you can afford any of these?"

Jen nodded, if a bit uncertainly. "Probably. I make decent money, I have quite a bit in savings because I don't ever spend very much and if I need to, I can probably use my house as collateral for a loan so I shouldn't have too much trouble getting one." She grinned over at Troy. "I'd have even more if I started charging you guys rent for staying with me."

Troy raised an eyebrow at her. "Let's not get too hasty, shall we?"

Jen snickered as she pulled up to the first house on the list. "It says this is a two bedroom, one and a half bathrooms, and has a den, so there should be plenty of room." She parked the truck and stepped out. "Let's have a look, hmm?"

As they walked around the house, looking in through the windows, Jen's hopes diminished. "That's not a bedroom," she grumbled, "that's a closet." She would barely be able to fit her bed in a room that size, let alone a pair of fully-grown men. She stomped back over to the truck and climbed inside. "What else have we got?"

Their next stop was at a townhouse and Jen didn't even bother to get out of the truck. "I'm pretty sure I could reach out through the side widow and touch the neighbor's house," she muttered as she glared at the house. "That's not privacy, that's claustrophobic."

The third house they stopped at was no better but at least Jen got out of the truck before deciding it wouldn't do. It had most of the key elements she was looking for but none of it seemed to fit together the way she would have liked. "If we can't find something better," she looked over at Troy, "then we can come back and have another look. But for now, I'm not sure I like this one."

After they left, Jen decided it was time to stop for lunch. She pulled into the first diner that they came across, hoping that the food tasted as good as it smelled from the parking lot. Inside, the restaurant was dark and warm and it reminded Jen of a few roadhouses she had been to when her parents had taken her and her siblings on vacation while the children had all been young.

A friendly waitress led her and Troy to a corner booth and while they waited for their food to arrive, Jen pulled out the realtor's list and set it on the table. "There has to be something in here," she muttered as she flipped past all the listings that had already been crossed out. "You can't have an entire town full of houses and have all of them suck."

She turned towards the higher end of her price range, hoping to find something more suitable there. After only a couple minutes, though, she tossed the list back onto the table. "I hate this." She dropped her head down onto her arms and sighed.

Troy gave her a sympathetic look and picked up the list. He flipped through the pages, scanning through the descriptions as he went. "What about this place?"

She lifted her head a couple of inches to see what he was talking about. "That's three bed-rooms; we don't need that much."

"No, but it's in your price range. Besides, I'm sure you'll find some use for the other room."

Jen nodded and dropped her head back onto the table. "Yeah, I can lock you guys in it when I need some peace and quiet."

Troy laughed at that. "Come on, the least you can do is have a look. Besides, it's cheaper than a couple of the other places you looked at, plus its closer to Sahara's place than the place you're at now."

"With my luck, it's probably haunted," Jen said, remembering how Angie had found a cheap place, only to discover too late that Eric already lived there. When she saw the expression on Troy's face, however, she relented. "Fine, we'll go look at it." She lifted her head just enough to glare at him. "Happy now?"

"Yes," he nodded. "But you might want to sit up, the food's here."

After they finished their lunch, they drove

over to the house that Troy had found. It was in a quiet, secluded section of town where the houses were set a short distance apart so that generous lawns stretched between them. The house itself was not overly large but it didn't seem to be too small, either.

They walked around the house, peering in through the windows and glass panels on the doors. "This isn't too bad," Jen finally admitted. "I wonder what's wrong with it."

Even Troy had to agree with her assessment. "Compared to the other places we looked at, this should be about a hundred, hundred fifty thousand more."

Still suspicious, Jen pulled out her phone and called Deborah. "I'm at the house on White Oak Lane, and I think there may have been a misprint in the listing."

On the other end of the phone, Deborah chuckled. "No, it's not a misprint. You're actually in luck because you're the first people to go out there and look at it."

"What's wrong with it? It seems awfully cheap."

"Tell you what, how about I come out with

the keys. You can have a look inside and I can tell you why the price is so low."

"Is it haunted?" Jen doubted it, but she had to ask. Although listing agents were required to disclose when a residence had a ghostly inhabitant, not all agents were sticklers for the rule, as Angie had learned the hard way.

"No, it's not haunted. I'll be there in half an hour, so just sit tight."

When Deborah arrived, she pulled up in a small maroon sedan. She smiled up at Jen and Troy, who were both sitting on the front porch. "Now don't the pair of you look nice? I think the house likes you."

Jen stood up and walked down the steps to meet her. "I like the house but I'm concerned."

"Understandably so," Deborah said as she pulled an enormous key ring out of her purse. "But believe me, there isn't really that much to distrust about this place." She led Jen and Troy up to the front door and opened it.

The entrance hall was bright and spacious, with peach and white tiles on the floor. Large glass panels over the front door kept the entryway brightly lit, even without turning on any lights. A small bench was built against one wall, perfect for sitting down on to remove muddy shoes. The living room was well-lit also, partly from the entrance and partly from the big bay windows that took up almost an entire wall. The floors were pale-colored hardwood, waxed and smooth.

The rest of the house was just as nice, with thick plush carpeting in the halls and matching tile in the kitchen and bathrooms. The bedrooms were upstairs and Jen was surprised to discover that not only was there a bathroom upstairs, but there was an enormous en-suite bathroom with a separate bathtub and shower area just off the master bedroom.

"Okay, why did you say this place was so cheap?" she turned to Deborah.

"The original owner of this house had it custom-built when he married his second wife. They lived here with his three children from a previous marriage. His wife passed away about two years ago and he followed her into the hereafter about three months ago."

"Does that mean it's haunted, then?" Troy interrupted.

She shook her head. "No. But none of the kids wanted the house and once it was out of probate, they all wanted it sold as quickly as possible so that they could each get their portion and go their own ways.

"It got out of probate the day before yesterday, so they wanted to put it well under market value so that it would sell faster." She looked around the upstairs landing. "Against my better judgment, I must say."

"So, no ghosts, then?" When Deborah shook her head with a smile, Jen asked, "and no other spirits? No poltergeists? Sagging roof, cracked foundation, skeletons buried in the backyard?" When Deborah continued to shake her head, amazement rolled over Jen.

"Okay, then. I guess I'll take it." Given the price of the house, she wouldn't even have to put her current residence up as collateral for the loan. She would, of course, just to make the whole process easier, but it was nice to know that she wouldn't have to overextend her finances to afford it.

By the time they got back home that evening, after filling out endless forms in Deborah's office, it was well past dark and Patrick was already there. He had placed a roll of carpeting against the wall beneath the new window. "I was just starting to wonder if I needed to send out a search party," he quipped as they walked inside.

"I bought a new house," Jen said as she walked towards the kitchen. Although she had dipped into the complimentary coffee in Deborah's office, her coffee had been rather weak and flavorless so Jen felt the need to brew a pot of real coffee.

Patrick dropped his tools and followed her into the kitchen. "You what?"

"I bought another house," she repeated. "It's up just past Sahara and Joel's place."

"Why?"

"Because I wanted a place that hadn't been on the news every night," she explained as she turned to face him. "One that doesn't smell like fire and burned carpeting and where the neighbors don't think I'm a werewolf."

Patrick took a step backwards. "Sorry," he said. "I hadn't realized you were that bothered by all this." He looked back over his shoulder at the supplies he had brought. "Does that mean you don't want me to fix the living room?"

"No," she sighed as she turned back to the coffeemaker. "I'm using this house as collateral on the loan for the new one, so it'd be better to have it in better condition when they come by to evaluate it."

"You're keeping this place after all, not just selling it once you get the new place?"

"Yep. I'm not sure if I'm going to rent it out, or what, but for now I want to keep it."

Patrick thought for a moment. "Well, if you decide you want to rent it out, I know of a few guys that could use a place."

Jen nodded. "Like I said, I haven't actually decided much but of you have someone that needs a place, they can stay here as soon as we move into the new place."

"I'm sure Paco will appreciate having a kitchen again. He's still raving about having been able to cook over here the other day."

"I had a feeling that's who you were talking about," Jen looked over at him. "And they're more than welcome to stay as long as they need to."

The next morning, after breakfast and a bit of waking up time, Jen started looking around her house, wondering how hard it would be to pack everything up when it was time to move. Deborah had told her that it might take over a week, maybe even two, to finalize everything, so she wasn't quite ready to pack yet. However, as she looked around her house, she realized that she didn't have all that much to move.

There was the mountain of mess in her bedroom and, of course, all of the furniture buried beneath it. There was a little bit of stuff in the living room but again not a lot besides her entertainment center. There were dishes in the kitchen and a few knickknacks scattered around but it surprised her to discover how little she actually owned.

Patrick had already removed the damaged couch, so there wouldn't be that to move. For now, he was sleeping on a blow-up mattress that he had purchased but Jen didn't figure it would be that difficult to move. Besides, she reminded herself, the mattress was Patrick's and therefore his problem.

That evening, she got another call from the

office. "Gear up," David said as soon as she answered the phone. "We've got action going on right now."

"Am I heading to the office or directly to the site?" she asked as she headed to get changed into her uniform.

"Head to the Eastern Mall. The rest of the team will meet you there; just get going as soon as you can."

"The mall?" Jen asked as she hung up the phone. "What's going on at the mall?"

By the time she got dressed and down to the Eastern Mall, the rest of the team had already gathered on the northwestern corner of the parking lot. As Jen pulled in to park next to them, there wasn't any point in asking what had happened.

Streams of people flowed out of every exit, running for their cars and trucks, the bus station, and even directly to the highway. A handful of police officers were in the middle of the crowd, trying unsuccessfully to calm the panicked people. What caught Jen's attention, however, was the enormous hole in the side of the building. To her, it looked exactly like the holes between houses at the last scene they had responded to.

Almost afraid of what she would find, she stepped out of her truck and headed for the building at a sprint. There was no way that she was going to be able to fight her way in through any of the exits because they were still over-crowded with all of the mall's patrons, who were desperately trying to escape. All she could hope for was that there wouldn't be too many bodies inside. She headed for the hole that the knights had left behind and darted into the building.

She had to climb over a couple piles of rub-ble, amazed at how much debris was left behind by a twelve-foot-tall hole in a wall. A couple of times, her feet slipped as the broken bits she was climbing over moved, but she made it in-side without too much trouble other than that.

Clothing racks, tossed aside by the crea-tures, were scattered everywhere. Broken per-fume bottles littered the floor and the stench of all the colognes mixed together was almost more than Jen's nose could handle. Further in, she could see the missing glass wall where the knights had exited the clothing store and moved deeper into the mall.

She followed the path of wreckage, the rest of the team close on her heels. In the next store, however, they found exactly what Jen had been afraid they would. Bodies, apparently tossed aside, were draped over the counters and display racks and scattered across the floor. Some of the bodies were missing appendages but at least none of them appeared to have been eaten.

In the next shop, they found more of the same. Bodies mixed with mannequins, creating a macabre display through the clothing store. A blood trail started there as well and Jen knew from hard-earned experience that the trail meant the knights had taken victims deeper into the mall.

In the corridors between stores, there was not as much carnage. It seemed as though most of the shoppers had been able to move out of the way of the marauding knights, so while there was still a lot of mess, most of it was non-human in nature.

The remnants of mayhem diminished as

they went further into the complex and Jen could only assume that by the time the monstrous creatures had gotten that far into the building, some sort of alarm had sounded and the patrons had started to move out of the area. There was still plenty of destruction, but there were very few bodies left to be found.

When they reached the other end of the mall, there was another hole leading outside. Through it, the team could see smashed cars, all in a line, heading directly away from the building.

"Should we follow it?" Ty asked as they looked out over the mess. "They're obviously gone but we might be able to pick out where they went."

Everyone agreed, so they set out on foot to find out where the path led. "Any bets," Mike called out once they were out of the parking lot, "on far do we think it'll be before the trail disappears this time?"

"Nope," J.J. answered. "It only goes about that far." He pointed a short distance away, where the damage simply stopped.

"What?" Jen jogged up to where the damage

ended. "They couldn't have just disappeared, that's not possible." A wide path of damage, bordered on both sides with dented and smashed vehicles, ended as abruptly as it had begun. Vehicles just past the trail of destruction waited in a tidy row, undamaged. She looked around, hoping for some sign that would show them which way the enormous knights had gone, but there was nothing. "It's not possible," she repeated, more to herself than anything else. "They have to have gone somewhere."

Even though the trail appeared to have gone cold, she insisted that they search the area more closely, certain that there would be a clue there, somewhere, that they hadn't noticed. She stepped closer to a compact car at the end of the trail that had been forcefully shoved aside and into neighboring cars.

When Marc suggested that they turn around and head back, she would have none of it. "We can't just let them get away again!" she howled. "Did you see what they did to those people? If we let them get away now, they'll just come back and do it again somewhere else. How many more people need to die because we couldn't stop them?"

"Don't you think I know that?" he responded. "But there's nothing here. Wasting our time looking it over again isn't going to change anything. All we can do now is hope that the people back at the mall have calmed down enough to tell us what they saw and clear the area so the ambulances can get in and maybe help some of them."

J.J. took Jen by an arm and led her back towards the mall. She followed, still seething. When they got back to the parking lot, they discovered that more police officers had arrived so the remaining crowd had calmed significantly. Medical teams were rolling in, leaving little for the New World team to do there.

Jen had no choice but to go home, although all she wanted to do was go back up behind the mall, find the tracks that she was certain were there, and trace the knights to whatever rock they kept crawling out from under. She would have gone up and done exactly that if it hadn't been for Mike, who followed her the entire distance back to her house. She wasn't entirely sure why he was following her but the best guess she could make was that either Marc or David had told him to, just in case she went off on her own as she was prone to do.

On one level, she understood that the team was doing what they were supposed to; since none of them had been able to find any signs of the knights leading further out of the area, all that was left for them was to wait and be ready the next time the knights showed up. That was the downside of being a response team instead of a strike unit. If New World was a strike team, their sole purpose would be to track the hellish knights and their pets to wherever they were hiding out in order to destroy them. On the other hand, she didn't care that she worked for a response team. There had already been too many people killed by these beasts and she wasn't sure she could handle the consequences of another attack.

When she arrived home, she parked in her driveway and stomped into the house, ignoring the response truck as it slowly cruised down the street. She would have slammed the door behind her, except she remembered that there was already enough damage to her living room and she didn't really think she needed to add a broken front door to the mess.

She stormed into the kitchen, swearing under her breath, and grabbed a bottle of water out of the fridge. Troy was already there, sitting at the kitchen table and watching the news. Jen ignored him, instead heading off to her bedroom to change out of her uniform.

When she came back to the kitchen, she was a little bit calmer, although not by much. She drank the last of her water and tossed the empty bottle towards her recycling bin, not even watching to see how close it came. She opened the fridge to see if there was anything to snack on, but the sound of the news report distracted her.

"Police have released that at least fifteen people were killed in today's attack but the body count continues to rise as more bodies are located. The responding units continue to make no headway in stopping these creatures, leading many to wonder where they will attack again. Some have wondered if this is more than

New World can handle because even though there have been multiple attacks by the same assailants, no progress has been made."

Jen stopped, leaned over in the refrigerator to listen. Slowly, she stood back up and closed the door before turning towards the television. "They want us replaced?" she asked, almost inaudibly. "What in the hell do they think that's gonna do? Who, exactly are they going to find that can track something that disappears into thin air?" Her voice steadily increased, both in pitch and in volume, until she was all but screaming. "They think they can find someone better? Nobody else has even come close to catching them!"

Troy jumped, startled by her outburst. "Hey, calm down," he stood up and stepped towards her.

"No! I'm not calming down! Those idiots think they can stand behind their cameras and talk shit, they don't even know the half of it!" Jen stepped away from him. "They haven't been out there, they haven't seen the bodies, they have no idea at all what we're up against!"

She started to pace as she ranted. "Hell, *we*

don't even know what we're up against, so how can they just sit there and say we're not doing anything? We're doing everything we can to stop those damned things and they just keep getting away, I don't understand it. There's no reason for that stupid bitch of a reporter to just stand there acting all smug and telling everybody that we can't do our jobs!"

Troy stood in front of her, an expression of shock on his face. Slowly, he backed out of the room, leaving her to rant in peace.

Jen paced across the kitchen, continuing to rant about the reporters and their obvious lack of intelligence. Soon, she heard a whispered conversation out in the living room but she was too absorbed in her anger to care. When Sahara came into the kitchen, Jen barely even noticed her, or Joel, who was a couple steps behind her.

Sahara walked around Jen, being careful to avoid getting in her path, and pulled her coffee mug out of the sink. Joel handed over a thermos, and Sahara poured a steaming liquid into the cup. Once it was filled, she offered it to her friend. "She'll be okay," she called over to Troy, who was peeking around the corner into the kitchen. "She's just a bit too stressed and needs to calm down a bit."

At first, Jen didn't realize that the cup she had been handed didn't contain coffee. She drank almost half of it before looking down. "What the..?" She glanced around the room, only then realizing that Sahara and Joel were there. "When did you get here?"

"Just a few minutes ago. You scared Troy, so he called us for backup."

As Jen nodded, Sahara indicated towards her cup. "Drink it," she said, "before it gets cold. It won't be nearly as good then."

Jen looked down at the cup in her hand again. In a single gulp, she downed the remaining tea. "What is this?"

"Just something to calm you down, that's all."

As the room started to sway around her, Jen heard Sahara's voice. "Joel, you want to catch her?"

She felt someone pick her up and carry her out of the room, and for a moment she wondered where she was going. She also heard someone that sounded a little bit like Sahara.

"Damn, I think the blend I gave her a was just little bit too potent."

# Chapter 10

When Jen woke in the morning, she wasn't entirely sure where she was. She sat up and looked around.

She was still dressed in the clothes she had changed into after getting home from the mall incident, which she hoped had only been the day before. She was sitting on a bed with a large, thick blanket draped over her. Another blanket was crumpled on the floor off to the side of the bed, as though she had thrown it off in the middle of the night. A nightstand and lamp were next to the bed and a low dresser sat against one of the walls. As Jen looked around, blinking to clear her eyes and her head, she realized that she was in Sahara's guest room.

She stood up and discovered that her sneakers were on the floor next to the bed. After stepping into them, she headed out to see where everyone else was.

She found Sahara in the kitchen, seated at the table with a pile of freshly cut herbs and a scale. Next to the scale were a stack of plastic bags, a sheet of pricing stickers, and a pen. As she weighed out precise amounts of the herbs, she poured them into a bag and wrote the weight and price on a sticker before sealing the pouch. When she realized Jen had entered the room, she looked up. "There's coffee made, go ahead and get some."

While Jen got herself a cup of coffee, Sahara measured out more herbs. "Do you feel better, at least?"

Jen nodded and had a seat at the table across from her friend. She took a sip of her coffee and watched as Sahara measured out more herbs from the slowly dwindling pile. "Yeah, thanks." She looked around the kitchen. "How did I get here?"

"Joel and I brought you back last night. You were in pretty bad shape."

As Jen thought about it, she vaguely remembered seeing Sahara and Joel at her house the previous night. "Was I that bad?"

Sahara nodded. "When he called me last night, Troy said you'd been pretty stressed out lately. He said this stuff's been bothering you a lot for a long time now. Why didn't you tell me?"

Jen shrugged. "I guess I just didn't want to bother you. I know you've had a lot going on lately, and I didn't think you needed me adding more to it."

"Dammit, Jen," Sahara looked up from her price sticker, irritation clearly written across her face. "Someone tried to set fire to your house and I find out about it on the five o'clock news? You have your new job, that's cool and all but now you're going out to murder scenes and wading through bodies, trying to catch the killer? A killer that probably isn't even human? And Troy says you're pissed off because you haven't found them yet. All of this on top of the crap that you've already had going on and you didn't want to *bother* me? What the hell?"

"Sorry," Jen apologized. "But I..."

"No," Sahara interrupted. "No buts. I shouldn't have had to go over to your house after Troy calls me in a panic because he thinks you've lost it." She looked up at Jen. "And you were damn close, I hope you know that."

Jen nodded, but stayed quiet. With how angry Sahara was at her already, the last thing she wanted to do was make it worse.

Finally, Sahara looked over at her and sighed. "Are you still tired?" When Jen shook her head, she asked, "Problems with your vision, any grogginess?"

"No, I feel fine."

"Good. I think the dose I gave you last night was a bit more than you needed so I just wanted to make sure you were okay."

When Sahara went back to her herbs, Jen got up and refilled both of their coffee cups before rummaging through the cupboards. She pulled out a pair of bread slices and stuck then into the toaster. While they were heating, she cut a couple slices of cheese.

Sahara looked up as Jen put the cheese between the pieces of toast. "What are you making?"

"Toasted cheese sandwich," she answered as she popped it in the microwave. She only cooked it for a few seconds, just long enough for the cheese to melt.

"You know," Sahara commented as Jen started to eat, "I'm starting to wonder who needs a babysitter more, you or the kids."

Jen looked up at her, surprised. "What?"

"Well, maybe not a babysitter, exactly, but I do think it's a good thing that you aren't living by yourself right now."

Jen blinked at her, confused. "Why's that?"

"Because you don't function well on your own, you never have. I just think it's better that you have someone with you to help keep an eye on you. You know, to make sure you eat, that you have clean clothes, stuff like that. Maybe even someone that can calm you down when you have a meltdown."

Jen shrugged. "Well, Troy's there and Patrick's there a lot of the time, too."

Sahara shook her head. "That's not what I meant. Troy's there because you need someone to watch your back, so for that, he's fine. But Patrick's there because he needed somewhere to stay and you're his sister. That's a little different. Neither one of them is going to be able to put you back together if you really start falling apart."

"This is starting to sound a lot like my mom's 'when are you getting married' speech." Jen said as she eyed her friend.

Sahara shook her head. "No, I'm not saying you need to run out and get married, that'd probably stress you out even more. But you really should work on finding someone that'll be there just for you. Not your brother, not your bodyguard, but just someone that you can lean on when you need someone." She grinned. "And if you can find one that cooks, even better."

After Jen finished eating and Sahara finished measuring out her herbs, Sahara drove Jen home. As Jen walked inside, she could tell immediately that there was something wrong.

New carpeting had been laid out in the living room, which she assumed was Patrick's handiwork. The stereo was playing but it was tuned into a country station that Jen never listened to and she had never heard Troy listen to it either. The volume was turned up and Jen was pretty sure that it could be heard from every room of the house.

She walked into the kitchen, carrying the box of leftovers that Sahara had sent home with her, and was almost blinded by how bright it was. The windows were more transparent than Jen had seen them since moving in and the room just smelled clean. When she opened the fridge to put away the food, she discovered that there might not have been enough room. Boxes and plastic containers were stacked inside the fridge so that Jen had to rearrange quite a lot of it to put her new additions away.

She walked back out of the kitchen and through the living room towards her bedroom. There, she found a pile of old, dirty clothes tossed out into the hallway just outside the door. Her closet was open and she could hear someone inside, rummaging around. Slowly and quietly, she crept towards her nightstand and pulled out her taser. "Whoever you are, come out of there, slowly."

A slight figure stepped backwards from the closet, an old dress of Jen's that she hadn't seen in years in her hands. The girl wore a powder blue and white striped sweater and blue jeans with colorful appliqués on the back pockets. Her curly hair was tucked behind both ears, further held out of her face by a slim headband.

When she turned around, Jen lowered the taser. "What are you doing here?"

Mary grinned at her. "Helping you clean your room. Patrick said you were moving and the place needed to be cleaned up before the assessors come by to decide how much collateral its worth." She tossed the dress onto another pile next to the bed. "Besides, this place was a wreck and needed to be cleaned out anyway."

"What does any of that have to do with my dress?" she gestured with the taser down at the garment on the pile.

Mary wrinkled her nose. "You've had that since high school. Do you even wear it?"

"Wait, you're getting rid of all of those?" Jen looked down at the pile, aghast. "Those are mine!"

"Don't worry," Mary said as she stepped back into the closet. "Jaime's out shopping for some new stuff for you right now."

"Oh, no," Jen whimpered as she sank onto the bed.

"Look," Mary stepped out of the closet, clothes in her hands. "We're just trying to help. Patrick said that you've been really busy lately and haven't been able to do much, so we all came over to pitch in. Jaime promised not to go too overboard and she'll even try to keep up with your style, or whatever you want to call it. Todd's out getting lunch, so he should be back pretty soon." She dumped the armload of clothes onto the bed and started to dig through them. "Patrick's at work right now but he said he'd be back after five."

Jen didn't even want to think about what fresh flavor of hell Jamie was dreaming up just then. Instead, she turned herself to the missing member of her strange little household. "Where's Troy? Shouldn't he be here, too?"

Mary shook her head. "He's down at your office, said he had a meeting with some guy named David. I'm not sure how long he'll be gone."

"David? My boss, David? Oh, crap!"

"Calm down, everything's fine," Todd called

out as he walked into the room. "There's burgers in the kitchen if you want one."

"No, everything's *not* fine," Jen looked over at her brother. "David's my boss; what's Troy doing in a meeting with him?"

"Talking about a couple of weapon ideas to help you guys take down those dark knights," Todd responded. "It sounds like you guys have been having a lot more trouble with them than I'd thought."

Jen nodded. "Yeah. It's like every time we get close, they disappear."

"That's what I had heard, too," Todd said. "But I got you something to cheer you up."

Jen raised an eyebrow at him.

"Ice cream," he explained. "With butterscotch topping."

"Yum," Jen exclaimed. "Where?"

"It's out in your freezer," he said as Jen sprinted out of the room.

When Jaime pulled up and parked in front of the house, Jen was still sitting at the kitchen table, eating the conciliatory ice cream. Jaime burst in through the front door and hollered for Todd and Mary. "I need a hand out here!!"

Jen groaned, not wanting to know how much new stuff Jaime had bought. She knew that everyone was just trying to be helpful and nice but she resented having her stuff gone through and half of it discarded when she wasn't even home to say anything about it. She also hated it when Jaime went shopping for her; she always tried to dress her in some new, trendy style that never looked good on Jen. The clothes were too expensive and they didn't last any longer than the cheap stuff Jen bought for herself.

Plus, most of the time, the cheap stuff was more comfortable.

She watched as Todd, Mary, and Jaime carried in load after load of shopping bags. When the trio went out for more, she dropped her head onto the table and tried not to scream.

"It's not that bad," Jaime called over when she noticed her sister's distress. "And not all of this is for you."

Jen blinked up at her. "Then what is it?"

Jaime grinned. "I went out to look at the latest on west coast fashions. That means that this entire trip becomes a work-related expense and I can write off a lot of it. For that to work,

I had to pick up a few things to take home with me but they're all in the same bags as your stuff.

"Aside from the stuff I got for research, I bought a couple of things for me, too. They're buried in all of it also."

Jen suspiciously peeked at the mountain of bags that she had brought over. "How did you fit all of that in your car? Your rental didn't look big enough to hold that much."

"It has a roomy trunk," Jaime explained as she opened one of the bags. "Here, you'll like this." She pulled out a jogging suit that was made out of a soft, fuzzy material. "It's velour," she explained.

Jen had to admit that it wasn't too bad and it looked a bit more comfortable than a lot of the stuff Jaime had gotten for her in years past had been.

"Like I told Mary, I'm trying to keep with your own individual sense of style, although in your case, it's more like a lack thereof. I just figured that you were due for a bit of an upgrade."

Jen nodded. "It's not as bad as I'd thought it would be," she admitted.

"And I noticed you'd chewed through most of your socks, too," Jaime said as she pulled something out of another bag.

They were socks, although not ones that Jen would have picked out for herself. They were thin, silky, and very pale pink. She looked at them doubtfully.

Jaime laughed as Jen searched for something to say. "Those are for me, I just had to see your face." She pulled out a handful of thicker socks and tossed them over. "I figured that these are more your style."

These were colorful and not as silky. Jen could tell they were made from the nice, sturdy cotton that she liked but the ends of them were strange. Instead of coming together in a nice, straight line as all of her other socks did, these ones had little tubes of fabric for each individual toe. "These are different," she said.

Jaime nodded. "I was surprised you didn't already have any. Those are so comfortable but they're best for just hanging around the house in."

All in all, Jen had to admit that a lot of the things Jaime had picked out weren't as awful as she had feared but she wasn't about to let Mary toss out all of her old clothes. "No, the new stuff isn't bad," she admitted, "but I got my clothes because I liked them."

She took the armload of clothes that Mary had been trying to sneak out to the trash bin and carried them back into her bedroom. "After they get washed, they'll be just fine."

When Troy got home, he was surprised at how many people were there. He blinked at the crowd for just a moment before walking over to Jen. "Should I leave?"

Jen shook her head. "No, its fine. They're just trying to help clean out the house."

He nodded. "I had an interesting meeting with Marc and David today."

"Yeah, Mary said that was where you'd gone."

"I gave them a few new ideas on weapons that should work better against those armored things, so that should make things a little bit easier for you." He grinned. "They want me to make up some more of my sticky bombs, the same ones we used on the portal."

Troy had used up the last of his explosives trying to destroy a magical gateway that led to the realm of dark energy known as Derathim. Since then, he had been talking about making more but hadn't quite gotten around to it. Now, it appeared he had an excuse to whip up some more.

Jen wasn't about to admit to him that there had been a point in time during her initial confrontation with the knights that she had been wishing for one of his explosives. She knew that would only encourage him, which was the last thing he needed, in her opinion. He was impossible enough to deal with as he was already.

When Patrick got home, he admitted to Jen that he had called the rest of the family to be there when she got home. "After what happened last night, I figured you shouldn't really be left all alone and I thought it'd be nice for you to have some time with them, too. Besides, Sahara had mentioned that she might have overdosed you and I wanted to be sure you were okay."

She appreciated that he was trying to help and she had to admit that it was nice seeing everyone again; she just wished that they would all calm down. Visiting is one thing but she didn't need them going through everything and trying to change it all.

By the time everyone left that night, Jen was exhausted. She crawled into bed, thankful that, at least for now, everyone was gone.

Almost as soon as her head hit the pillow, however, her phone rang. She barely even opened her eyes as she growled into the receiver. "What?"

"My apologies, it appears that I have woken you again."

The voice on the other end sounded familiar, but she couldn't quite place it. "Who is this?"

"I have decided where we should meet, as you agreed. There is a coffee shop just up the road from the museum, off of Eighteenth Street. If you could meet me there in an hour, I will be waiting."

As he spoke more, she was able to figure out that he was the thief she had agreed to help. "An hour?" She looked over at the clock, which read ten thirty. "Are you serious?"

"Quite serious. I would prefer that you come alone but I don't truly expect you to do so.

However, I think it would be best if we could keep this as quiet as we could; I don't want to call too much attention to our meeting. I have no idea how many spies my daughter's captor has and I don't want to do anything to jeopardize her."

"What about the person that's been after me? I thought you had said you could produce him."

"And so I shall. He will be forthcoming once our meeting is concluded."

With a sigh, Jen agreed. "I'll be there. I hope you appreciate this."

"Oh, I do indeed. And I will make it worth your while, I assure you." As before, once he was finished speaking, the line went dead.

"Ah, hell," Jen grumbled as she climbed out of bed. "It's like he knows I don't want to deal with this right now." She padded out to the living room, where both Patrick and Troy were still awake. They were sitting on the new carpet in front of the television, which had been moved back into the living room, playing video games. "Game over," she said, looking down at Troy.

"I thought you were going to bed," he said as he paused the game.

"I was, but I got another call. You feel up to backup?"

"Sure, what's up?" He dropped the controller and pushed himself to his feet. "More armor things?"

"No, this is a side thing I agreed to help someone out with. You know the coffee shop off eighteenth, down by the museum?"

Troy thought for a moment. "I think so. What's there?"

"I will be, in about an hour. But I want you there ahead of me so I know you're already in place when I get there."

He raised an eyebrow at her. "Sounds pretty cloak-and-dagger. Want to let me in on it?"

"Remember the thefts that have been all over the news?" When he nodded, she said, "I'm on my way to meet the thief."

"You're what?" Even Patrick looked up at her announcement.

Jen nodded. "He says he's being forced to do the robberies and he offered to hand over the jackass that's been trying to kill me if I meet with him. So that's where I'm headed."

"Are you crazy? What if he's the guy after you? You could be walking into a trap!"

"You think I don't know that?" she whirled on her brother. "Why do you think I wanted Troy there ahead of me?" She looked from Patrick and over to Troy. "Understand now?"

His smile gone, the hybrid nodded. "I'm on my way. I should be there in about fifteen minutes, so that'll be plenty of time to scope the place out. If it's a trap, I'll let you know as soon as I can."

"Good enough."

"Wait," Patrick climbed to his feet. "I'm going with you."

"No. He wanted me to go alone and it's risky enough just sending Troy. If you go too, it'll just make it more dangerous."

Over Patrick's objections, Troy left and Jen headed back into her bedroom to get dressed. As she pulled her pistol out of the locked box she kept it in, she hoped she wouldn't have to use it. Once she was ready, she checked her clock again. She would have to leave in about twenty minutes to be there at the agreed-upon time.

Patrick was still in the living room when she left. He made one last attempt to get her to agree to take him with her for the meeting but she refused and left without him. As she drove to the coffee shop, she hoped that Troy had managed to get into place successfully and that she had been overly prepared for nothing. She doubted it, but it was a nice thought.

She parked on the street out in front of the shop and looked around. Through one of the windows, she could see Troy, sitting nonchalantly at a small table and, to all appearances, reading one of the shop's complimentary newspapers. There didn't appear to be many other patrons at the shop, no surprise considering how late it was, so she was glad she hadn't brought Patrick. His presence would have been even more obvious than Troy's.

She stepped out of the truck and headed inside. There, she ordered a drink at the counter and sat at another small table. While she waited, she looked at the other customers, wondering who her mystery man was.

At one table, near the one Troy was at, a pair of young women sat, eagerly discussing something that sounded suspiciously like a college class. Since they were both female, Jen doubted that either of them was her caller. However, she also suspected that they were the reason Troy had chosen his seat.

A middle-aged man sat at another table, listlessly tapping at the keyboard of his laptop computer. A handful of paper cups sat on the table nearby, testament to the fact he had been there a while.

After only fifteen minutes, a man that she hadn't noticed walked over to sit at her table. He was dressed in faded blue jeans and a white shirt under a black leather jacket. He was quite a bit shorter than Jen, she guessed him to be about Mary's height. He had short, light brown hair and rich brown eyes.

"Quite pleased you could make it on such short notice," he greeted her. Only then did she realize that this was actually the man she had been expecting.

She also realized that, as he spoke, she could

see a glint of fang between his lips. "You're a vampire?"

He nodded and smiled, careful to not expose too much of his teeth. "You were expecting something else, I see. Don't worry, I am legal. There is no worry about that." In order for a vampire to remain legal, he had to be registered with both the county and at least one local blood bank. Since they weren't allowed to feed off of humans, willing or otherwise, donor blood was their only option. Because of that, all a vampire had to do was approach any blood bank, show his fangs, and he would be allowed to eat. The government had regulated that a number of years ago, just after vampirism had become removed as a reason for extermination.

Jen shook her head. "It's not even that I was expecting something else, but you don't seem like the vampires I've seen."

He chuckled. "Not all vampires are tall and anorexic with a bad French accent."

"Sorry, I hadn't meant that." she looked over her coffee cup at him. "I don't even know what to call you."

"You can call me William. That is the name I have been using for many years now." He looked around the café for a moment before turning back to her. "I may not have much time, so we need to discuss this quickly." He folded his hands on the table and leaned forward. "Since I was told to be as honest with you as I could be, I shall make this as succinct as I possibly can. My daughter, Rachel, was stolen from me over a month ago. I spent the first couple weeks trying to find out who had her but finally realized only recently that this was not something I could do on my own. In short, I needed help.

"Before you ask, no, this isn't a simple kidnapping with an amusing ransom. I am afraid that my involvement is only the tip of the problem and a possible attempt to get me out of the picture."

"Wait," Jen interrupted. "I thought vampires couldn't have kids."

He chuckled. "There are two parts to that question. First of all, vampires can have children. It is frowned upon because there are quite a lot of problems with the process and the possibility of survival for both mother and child is low. However, in cases such as mine, if the children are born before the parent is turned, that vampire will indeed have children."

"I hadn't realized you were a new vampire. I had been under the impression that you were a lot older."

"I am. I was turned over a hundred years ago."

"Then how could your kids be alive?" Jen looked over at him in confusion. "Or were they turned, too?"

"Neither. Rachel was quite the powerful sorceress in her day. After I was turned, she spent all of her time trying to find a cure, to turn me back into a human."

"That's not possible, is it?"

He shook his head. "Not that I have ever seen, no. But Rachel thought she was onto something. She had planned on trapping the vampire, the part of me that was infected, in a soul gem. By that time, I was desperate and agreed to try her experiment.

"But something went wrong. Instead of drawing out the vampiric essence from me and absorbing that into the gem, her spirit was drawn out instead. Since that day, I have carried

Rachel with me in the hopes that one day I would find a way to restore her."

"And that's what was stolen?"

William nodded. "Yes. And unless I do as instructed, she will be destroyed, lost forever."

"Do you know who stole her, or where she is being held?"

He shook his head. "I had hoped to find out by now, to at least have that much information for you, but I'm afraid I am at a loss. The only thing I can tell you is that my orders come to me from a powerful demoness."

Jen sat back at his statement. The last thing she wanted to get tangled up in was another mess with demons but she couldn't help but feel for the vampire. She couldn't imagine how much pain he must be in. Not only had he lost his daughter once, in one of the most horrifying ways Jen could imagine; now she had been taken from him again. "So where can I find this demoness?"

He lowered his head. "That is another piece of information that I do not have."

"In that case, what can you tell me? Maybe

there is something else that will lead us in the right direction."

"I'm not sure what else I have that will help. I can tell you that the first thing I was ordered to steal was jewelry; I believe you already know about that." When Jen nodded, he continued. "And then there was the museum heist; I'm still not sure why she wanted that."

"What did you take from there? Information about that hasn't been released yet." she asked. "The news hasn't even released what exhibit anything was taken from."

"It was an Aztec exhibit. I stole a shaman's breastplate and what is believed to have been a sacrificial dagger crafted of obsidian stone."

Jen's brows furled as she thought about this. "What would a demon want with those?"

William shrugged. "I know that long ago these were used in ritual sacrifice, but I know of no further significance."

"And next was the Tiara, right?"

"Correct, although I am not certain of the significance of that item, either. Granted, it was a beautiful piece, most likely worth a lot of money, but I cannot fathom why a demon would want it."

"And that's all you've taken?"

William nodded. "Although I have been given another task, I am hoping that you will rescue my Rachel before I am to complete it."

"What are you supposed to get next?"

"I'm not sure, but I know that it's going to be difficult. There's a box that the NPIB has in their storage vault, item number 4619-D. She wants me to bring her that box with the seal still intact. I'm not sure what that means, but I'd hazard a guess that there is something very dangerous inside."

"And she didn't tell you what it was? Nothing more about it but the item number?"

William shook his head. "That's all she gave me." He looked around the coffee shop for a moment before continuing. "I could probably delay it by a couple days, the NPIB archives can't be that easy of a place to break into, but I do fear what might happen if I do." He visibly shuddered at the idea. "Nor do I wish to be anywhere near her if she does manage to get her claws on that box, whatever it may hold."

Jen sighed. "I'll see what I can do." She took another drink of her coffee. "You should know, though, that I'll probably have to bring in my team on this one. I may be good but even I can't take out a demon on my own."

"I understand that and I appreciate your discretion in this matter."

"You should also know that if I find out you've been lying to me, or if you double-cross me in any way, that would be a very big mistake on your part."

He smiled at her. "My dear, I understood that before I called you the first time. As I have said, I understand the need to be perfectly honest with you."

She nodded. "There's also a very real chance that you'll still end up in prison for a very long time after all this is over with. There will come a time where I have to report who you really are."

"I understand that." he stood up. "And since it appears that we have come to an understanding, I believe I have something you want." He turned to head for the door. "If you would follow me, please."

Jen resisted the urge to shoot a look at Troy

as she stood up to follow him outside. Only a couple of steps later, however, William looked over at her. "You may want to bring your friend outside with you as well; he appears displeased at the prospect of your leaving with me." He looked directly at Troy and nodded.

With neither denial nor further invitation, Troy stood up and followed them outside.

William led them over to a nondescript green sedan in the parking lot. When they arrived, he pulled a key from his pocket and opened the trunk. Inside, cramped into the small space, was the man that had tried twice to kill Jen.

He was unconscious, but it was easy to tell that he was still alive. He groaned slightly as Troy lifted him out of the trunk. "Looks like a plan to me," the hybrid said as he carried the limp body over to the back of his own car. He reached down and unlocked the truck, then thought a moment as he realized that his trunk was too full to fit anything more inside.

He looked over at Jen's truck. "That won't work," he said. "You don't even have a trunk." A grin slowly spread across his face as he stepped closer to the Jeep. "But you do have a brush guard."

"No," Jen stepped in front of him, knowing what the hybrid had in mind. "You aren't sticking him on the front of my truck."

"Just think," he stopped to tell her, "You wouldn't even have to worry about tailgating anyone on the way."

She stood in front of him, arms folded and shaking her head. "Not gonna happen. I want him to have a long, adventurous life behind bars." She smirked. "With an enormous cellmate named Bubba."

"Fine." Troy turned back towards his car. "Are you taking him to the station, or am I?"

"I'll take him but if you want to follow me there, I'd appreciate it."

Troy set the man down on the ground next to the still-open trunk. As he rummaged around inside, Jen looked over towards William. "I'll see what I can find out about your daughter and your situation. Until then, just don't do anything that'll get you into trouble."

"I shall do my best," he answered as he

climbed into his car. "I hope to speak with you again soon, hopefully on better terms the next time."

"Wait, there is one more thing that I am curious about."

"What's that?"

"Who told you to call me? You've mentioned a few times that you were told I was the best person to talk to but you never told me who said that."

William smiled wryly. "I'm not sure whether or not you will believe it but a man came to me in a dream."

Jen watched him drive away before turning back to Troy. "What are you doing?"

"If he's riding with you, I want to make sure he isn't going to break free halfway there," Troy answered as he wrapped another strip of duct tape around the unconscious man. Somehow, in the short period of time that Jen had taken her eyes off him, Troy had managed to mummify their captive in silvery tape. From toes to shoulders, he was completely covered. "Look, he even has handles," Troy said as he pointed to a couple of extra flaps that hung off the mummy's sides.

# Chapter 11

Jen had planned on taking their captive to the closest police station but about halfway there she changed her mind. Instead, she pulled out her phone and called David. "Hey, who's at the office right now?" she asked as soon as he answered.

"Standard night shift crew," he answered. "Why?"

"I've got the jackass that's been trying to kill me in the back of my truck and I was figuring on dropping by the office. Do we have somewhere to put him until morning?"

"You what?" The grogginess that had been apparent in David's voice vanished. "Just wait there, I'm on my way."

"You got it," she smirked as she hung up. For

all the times she had been woken up when she was tired, sometimes it felt good to spread the joy around to others.

She and Troy waited in the New World Response parking lot until David's familiar sedan pulled into the lot. Jen grinned into his headlights and waved him over.

"How did you get him?" David asked as he climbed out of his car. "Last I heard, the police had no leads and the watch I had put on your house hasn't turned up anything either."

"You put a watch on my house?" Jen was surprised; she hadn't known about that. "A friend turned him over to me." She popped open the cargo area of her truck and stepped aside so that David could see. "I have no idea how long he'll be out, so we might want to get him inside."

David gaped at the man in the back of her truck. "What happened to him?" He finally asked.

"Troy wanted to be sure that he wouldn't get free; he was riding with me, after all."

David shook his head. "Okay." He looked

over at Troy. "You want to bring him inside? Once we get the tape off him, we can turn him over to the police." He directed his attention back over to Jen. "Speaking of the police, why didn't you turn him over to them?"

Jen shrugged. "First, I'm still not sure I can trust all of them. They already let him escape once and I knew I could trust you guys."

"Besides," she added, "I needed to talk to you about a couple things anyway so I figured it'd be easier to just get it all taken care of at once."

As they followed Troy inside, David asked, "What's on your mind?"

"Well, there are three things, and I'm not sure how much you're going to like any of them."

"So how about you start with one and we'll go from there?"

She nodded and gestured towards Troy and his captive. "First, there's the friend I got him from."

"Somehow I knew there was going to be more to that story." David held a door open for the others to walk through. "Go ahead and put him down in here. I'll have someone come up to get the tape off in a few minutes."

Troy nodded and dropped his load onto the floor. As they walked back out of the room and David locked it behind them, Jen explained about William and how she got involved with him. "He knows he's going to get some prison time but if he's telling the truth about his daughter, I have to help."

"Did he explain how he was able to get past all those security systems to take what he stole? According to everything I've heard, some of those were supposed to be virtually impossible."

Jen shook her head. "I didn't think to ask. But that all leads me to the second thing I wanted to discuss with you."

"What's that?"

"You had mentioned a while ago that there was a database that the NPIB maintains over all the paranormal activity that gets reported to them, right?" When David nodded, she said," Is there any way you could get me access to that?"

He stopped and turned to face her. "What do you need that for?"

"William said that the next thing he was after is in the NPIB archive vault. I figured that if we knew what he was supposed to be stealing, it might give us a better idea of what's going on."

He shook his head. "I don't even have access to that type of information. If the NPIB has something in storage, it's usually for a damn good reason. Even with everything else your new friend has already done, I'm not sure he'll be able to pull off something like that."

She nodded her agreement. "I hadn't figured he'd be able to either. I may not know much about their vault but I'd figured that if they have something stashed away, it's probably guarded better than just about anything else out there."

"Sorry, but there really isn't any way I can get that information, at least not quickly. I can make a couple calls and see what I can do, but no promises."

"I was more or less expecting as much." She thought for a moment. "What about finding people? Can we do that?"

"If you're asking if they have some sort of

record that'll show where this Rachel is, then no."

Jen shook her head. "I need to talk to the dreamwalker."

The dreamwalker was a psychic who had been possessed by a demon up until a short time ago. He had contacted Jen because he was trapped and couldn't free himself, so he had requested that she kill the demon, even at the cost of his own life. She had managed to remove the demon from the dreamwalker without killing him but hadn't heard from him since. Now, however, since William said that he was contacted in a dream, she thought that it was fairly likely that it was the same dreamwalker reaching out to her for help again.

David sighed. "Yeah, I suppose I could get that. You really think he can help?"

She shrugged. "I think he's already involved. I just want to talk to him and see how much he really knows."

He nodded thoughtfully. "Technically, I think he's still listed as one of our cases, so I should be able to find out where he is. I'm not sure how happy people are going to be about you looking for him, though. You did a number on him the last time you saw him."

That was an understatement. She had used the clue-by-four, the magical wooden post that Todd had enchanted for her, to remove the demon from the man. Unsurprisingly, it had done some damage to the man that persisted once he and the demon were separate.

"At least he's alive; he'd told me to kill him. That should count for something."

"Let me see what I can do. Is there anything else?"

Jen thought for a moment. "No, I think that about covers it. I had told William that I would try to keep from turning him in until we got his daughter. I want to stick with that, because you never know when we might need something more from him and if he's locked away, he might be less willing to help." She didn't really expect William to become unwilling to assist in the search for his daughter if he was incarcerated but she had strong reasons to believe that her access to him under such circumstances would be limited.

"That makes sense," David agreed. "I'll make some calls and let you know what I find out tomorrow. You should go home and get some sleep, though. You look terrible."

Jen and Troy headed home after that, leaving the hapless would-be assassin in David's capable hands. Patrick was waiting at the house, eager to hear about the meeting. Jen left Troy to fill him in on the story while she headed in to bed.

When she woke in the morning, she felt a lot better. Her phone had remained blessedly silent for the remainder of the night and the guys had at least kept their noise level down to a dull roar, a first since they had both been there. She could smell the coffee as she opened her eyes and even though she knew she hadn't set the pot she was thankful that at least someone had remembered.

She was halfway through her first cup when there was a knock at the front door. Both Troy and Patrick were still fast asleep in the living room, so she went out to see who it was.

J.J. stood on the front porch, hands in his pocket and hunched over in the cold. "Damn, it's getting worse every day," he said as she let him inside.

Jen shrugged. "Winter happens, I guess. Coffee?"

He accepted the offered cup, holding the mug in both hands to absorb some of the warmth into his frozen hands. "My car was iced over this morning; otherwise, I would have been here a little bit earlier."

She chuckled at that. "I guess that was a good thing then, because I wouldn't have been up when you got here and you would have ended up waiting outside for a while." She dropped a pair of waffles into the toaster. "What's up?"

"David said you were asking about where the dreamwalker is. He got the information this morning but the NPIB guys don't want to let you in with him alone so David sent me down to come with you."

Jen looked up in surprise. "Why don't they want me alone with him? It's not like I'd hurt him or anything."

J.J. shrugged. "Apparently they aren't seeing it that way." He took a drink of his coffee. "But he's down at the long-term-care ward at North Bank Hospital."

"What's he doing in there?" Jen asked as she spread peanut butter across her waffles. "All I thought he had was a broken arm."

"I don't know, but that's where he's supposed to be. Do you want to go or not?"

"Yeah, just let me get dressed," she said as she took a bite of her breakfast. "I'll be right back."

Once she was dressed and had finished her waffles, they headed out to his truck. Jen initially protested but J.J. pointed out that his truck was already warmed up so they wouldn't be frozen for as long. Reluctantly, Jen had to concede his point.

It didn't take too long to get to the hospital, which gave Jen some time to reflect on how much time she had been spending there lately. They walked towards the ward where the dreamwalker was supposed to be and Jen asked, "So which room is he supposed to be in?"

"I don't know," J.J. answered, "we'll have to ask at the nurse's station."

When they got there, there was only one person on duty. She looked up as the pair approached. "Can I help you?"

"We're here for Steve Jenkins," J.J. pulled out his badge and showed it to her. "I believe you're expecting us."

She took the badge and examined it, looking over at Jen with slightly narrowed eyes. "Right this way," she said as she handed it back to J.J. and stepped around the counter.

"I'm not sure how much you hope to accomplish," the nurse explained as she led them down a hallway. "He's been in a coma since arriving here and the doctors aren't expecting that to change any time soon." She stopped in front of a door. "He's inside. Go ahead and take your time; he doesn't get too many visitors and I doubt he'll mind the company." She opened the door and allowed them inside.

Jen stepped into the room and looked at the man lying under the thin blanket. His beard had grown slightly since she had last seen him, now tinged with a hint of grey. She walked over to the side of his bed, astonished at how much smaller he had gotten in only a short time. He hadn't been overly large to begin with but now he looked positively frail. Cautiously, she sat on the edge of the mattress, careful not to disturb any of the electronics that led from his body to the array of machines that stood nearby, and took one of his hands in her own.

"I don't know if you can hear me," she said gently, "but it's me, Jen." She looked around at the monitors, all of which were recording everything that he was going through. She didn't know what she was looking for but she had hoped that there would be some sign that would indicate that he had heard her and knew she was there.

"I spoke to William," she said, again without response. "I've agreed to help him. I think you were the one who sent him to me, so I thought you'd want to know that."

She looked closely at his face as she spoke but he didn't even twitch an eyelid. With a sigh, Jen accepted that he probably wasn't going to respond to her but there were things that she wanted to tell him, just in case he could hear her. "We found the portal you warned us about and we destroyed it. There's no way left for the demon to come back and find you."

She explained about what it had taken for the magical gate to be broken but there was still no response. Finally, she turned to J.J. "I don't know what else to say."

J.J. nodded. "Maybe it'd be best if we left for now. If he heard you, he knows what's going on and maybe that'll be enough for him to wake up. If not, we can always come back later. I'm sure that it won't be too hard to get a visitors' pass."

Jen nodded and stood up, carefully setting the dreamwalker's hand back onto the bed. "I'll come back," she promised. "As soon as I'm done, I'll let you know what happened."

She followed J.J. out of the room and back out to the nurse's station, where the same woman was still on duty. "You said he's been in the coma the whole time he's been here?" Jen asked the nurse.

She nodded. "I believe the police brought him in as soon as they got him and he hasn't re-gained consciousness. The doctors had initially hoped that he would have come to on his own but now they aren't so sure that he ever will."

"Do you have any psychics on staff?" Jen asked.

"Yes, of course we do. Why?"

"Because he's a dreamwalker, that's why. He's been communicating since being here, so maybe if you can find a psychic that can reach him, it'll give him a better chance of waking up."

"How do you know that?" the nurse asked.

"Because I'm one of the people he contacted not too long ago, and I have reason to believe that he's been in contact with someone else too. That was the reason we came today, to find out more about the other person he's been talking to."

The nurse tapped at a computer that was tucked behind the desk. "There's no record in here of him being a psychic."

"Well, he is, so you might want to make a note of that."

The nurse nodded. "That would explain some of the strange readings we've been getting from him, too."

"Strange readings?" Jen asked. "Like what?"

"Well, there have been a few times when the cerebral monitors have picked up a change in activity," she explained. "The doctors thought that meant that he was waking up but they always stopped with no physiological change that we've been able to identify." She looked up at Jen and J.J. "I really should notify someone of this. I'm sure you can see yourselves out."

As the two of them left, Jen was pleased to see that the nurse had picked up a phone and was calling someone, hopefully either a doctor or the on-staff psychic.

"So where to next?" J.J. asked.

Jen only thought for a moment. "Sugar and Spice." It was already late enough in the morning that she was certain the shop would be open.

"What's that?"

"It's Sahara's herbal shop. She has something there that I think I need."

"Okay," J.J. agreed, "but you're going to have to tell me how to get there."

Jen had no trouble directing J.J. to Sahara's shop. When they got there, Jen headed inside, feeling the familiar warmth that Sahara had imbued into her shop, which had nothing to do with the heater settings. "Remember that tea you made for me a while ago to help with the nightmares?" she asked when she found her friend.

Sahara nodded. "The Dreamless blend. Are you having nightmares again?"

"Well, yeah, but that's apart from what I want the tea for. Last time, every time I used it, the dreamwalker was able to get in touch with me. I'm starting to think that he can't reach me without it for whatever reason."

"You know, it doesn't work that way," Sahara explained as she pulled a packet off of a shelf and tossed it over. "All this stuff does is help to remove dreams, not to let the psychics in."

"I know that's not what it's supposed to do," Jen admitted, "but the only time the dreamwalker was able to talk to me was when I was using the tea. Maybe he couldn't get past the nightmares or maybe I was just sleeping better which made it easier for him to reach me, I don't know. But it's got to be worth a shot."

"What's going on now?" Sahara asked.

"It's a long story." At the look she got from

that, Jen decided that it would be better in the long run to tell her friend everything. She explained about the vampire thief and his daughter, and about the demoness that held her. She also explained that the vampire had called her because he was told to in a dream but when she and J.J. had gone to go see the dreamwalker, whose name she had finally learned was Steve Jenkins, they found him in a coma. "So, you see, this might be the only way for me to figure out what's going on."

With a sigh, Sahara waved her off. "You're going to get yourself into real trouble one of these days, you know. Have you told anyone what you're up to?"

"Of course. There have been people with me every step of the way." She looked out the window behind her. "In fact, J.J. is out in the truck right now."

"Okay," Sahara sighed, "but whatever you're getting yourself into, you'd better start being a bit more careful."

"I will," Jen promised. "But I really should go."

There wasn't a lot more running around that needed to be done that day, so after J.J. dropped her off at her house Jen spent most of the remaining time packing. There was only a little while left before she was supposed to move into her new place and her family had brought over a lot of new stuff that she was now going to have to pack. Luckily, Troy had picked up an entire stack of cardboard moving boxes for them to use.

At least Troy and Patrick would be easy to move, she thought to herself as she dumped more stuff into the boxes she had dragged into her bedroom. Both of the guys still lived out of their suitcases and duffel bags, so packing would be no problem for them. She, on the other hand, still had a lot of stuff that she needed to get ready to go.

That night, she fixed up a cup of the Dreamless tea she had gotten from Sahara, hoping that her plan would work. She knew that the tea wouldn't automatically put her into contact with Steve Jenkins but at that point, she was willing to try just about anything.

She crawled into bed early, remembering how tired she always felt after a lengthy visit with the dreamwalker. For some reason, although she was asleep during all of their conversations, she always felt as though she hadn't slept at all afterwards and she wanted to make sure that there would be enough time for her to get some rest later on in the night after their conversation was completed.

Besides, she told herself as she pulled the blankets up over her, even if it didn't work, she could probably use a good night's sleep. Preferably one without dreams filled with people being torn apart by black knights and their monstrous horses.

She had no idea how long she had been asleep, whether it was minutes or hours, but soon enough she found herself standing outside. She was in the middle of a field, the same field in which she normally met with the dreamwalker, but instead of being covered by grass and flowers as it had been the last time she was there, she was almost knee-deep in snow. The faint moonlight glittered off the frozen landscape, making everything much brighter than it would have otherwise been.

Steve was there waiting for her, just as she

had expected him to be. He smiled when he saw her and walked towards her, barely leaving any footprints in the snow. "I was wondering how long it would take you to get here," he said as he stopped a few feet in front of her. "I've been waiting."

Jen looked over at the man. He looked as she remembered him, whole and healthy, not the deflated caricature he had seemed to be in the hospital. "I came to visit you in the hospital," she said. "I hadn't known you were still there."

He nodded. "It seems like I have been there for quite some time but I'm sure it hasn't been as long as it feels." He stepped closer. "I understand William has been to see you?"

Jen nodded. "I figured you'd sent him."

"I did, yes. His situation is unique, so I knew of no better person to trust him to. I'm sure that with you, he's in good hands."

"Thanks, I think." She looked around the clearing, surprised she wasn't cold in the snow. Normally she'd be absolutely freezing by then, but her breath wasn't even making the normal billows of steam as she breathed. "But he doesn't know where his daughter is and there isn't really a whole lot I can do to help him without that."

"I am aware of that but I am certain that you will come up with something that will help."

"But how?" she asked him. "If I don't know where his daughter is, then I can't go get her back for him and the demon's going to keep making him steal stuff until he gets caught."

"Has he told you the significance of who his daughter is?"

Jen shook her head, confused. "All he told me was that she was a mage."

He nodded. "Your brother is a mage as well, is he not?" When she nodded, he said, "How powerful must a mage be in order to create a spell such as the one she created? A Soul Gem is no easy feat."

"I don't know, pretty powerful, I'd guess." Before her conversation with William, she had never heard of a Soul Gem but Todd was probably already familiar with them. Why hadn't she thought to ask him about it while he'd been visiting?

"Powerful, indeed. In her day, she was the

single most powerful user of magic in the world. Now, how valuable would a person such as that be to a demon?"

Jen had already understood, at least on a basic level, that Rachel had been a powerful magic user in her time, but she hadn't realized that she was the most powerful. She couldn't quite wrap her brain around what that would mean, but it did bring up a different train of thought. "I can understand that she's really powerful," she admitted, "but what good would it do for a demon to have a trapped mage, regardless of her power level? She can't use her magic while she's in the gem, can she?"

"No," the dreamwalker agreed, "she cannot. However, should she be freed, she will discover that her powers have continued to grow during her time in isolation."

"I thought there was only a set amount that a person is born with, so how can her power grow?"

"Normally that is true, but her case is unique. She has been in constant contact with a very powerful artifact for a great many years now. The more contact a person has with any sort of magical energy, the more of that energy they absorb into themselves. In effect, her entrapment has caused her magical power to increase many times over during her captivity in a most unnatural way."

Jen nodded. "That's why you think the demon wants to release her, so that it can use her power?"

"It sounds like a reasonable theory, does it not?"

She thought about it for a moment. "That means it really doesn't matter if I stop William from having to keep stealing because that's not what the demon's really after. What I need to do is stop the demon from releasing Rachel so that it isn't able to use her power for itself."

"Correct. If there is a way to release her, it would likely be a good idea to do so; just not where the demon can get to her."

Jen sighed. "That still doesn't help me to find either her or the demon but no matter how I look at it, I'll need to find them both."

Steve paced across the snow, still not making very many tracks. "I am reluctant to tell you any more about the demoness that has the

Soul Gem. She is very powerful and I am not certain that I am willing to put you in that much danger."

"Then why did you send William to me?"

"He needed someone that would listen and who would believe his tale. However, I believe you need to contemplate who you will bring with you very closely. The demoness has many traps and I don't want either you or your friends to fall prey to any of them."

"I was planning to take Troy, if he wants to go, and my team. Same as I did when I came after you."

He stopped pacing and turned back towards her. "She lives in a heavily guarded mansion, a distance from where you live. But I warn you again to be careful, for she is intelligent and far trickier than the demon that had me."

Jen nodded. "I'll be careful and I'll tell the rest of the group to keep their eyes open, too."

Once he was satisfied that she intended to go after the demon and the Soul Gem, he explained to her how she could find the demoness. "She is not in an underground complex such as the one you found me in," he explained.

"This time you and your team will be out in the open, so you will face an entirely new set of dangers."

"What about you?" she asked. "You've been in a coma for a while. Are you going to wake up any time soon?" She looked at him more closely. "*Can* you wake up?"

He smiled at her reassuringly. "The doctors can call it a coma if they like. Personally, I call it a long, well-deserved nap."

"Okay, then," she said. "But you might want to think about waking up soon. For one, you look terrible. You know how bad hospital food can be, right?" When he smiled at her, she grinned back at him. "And for two, sometimes it's just easier to use the phone when you need to talk to someone."

# Chapter 12

When she woke in the morning, she was a lot more refreshed than she had expected to be. She climbed out of bed, surprised at how brightly the sun was shining through her window. When she looked over at the clock, she understood why; it was almost noon.

She climbed out of bed and headed for the kitchen. As she walked through the living room, she noticed that Patrick had already gone to work. She nodded at Troy, who was sitting at the dining room table with a handful of glass jars and a couple of metal tubes. He barely looked up as she walked into the room. "How'd it go?"

Jen shrugged and yawned as she poured a cup of coffee that was still lukewarm. She could tell that it had been made a few hours ago but it was still caffeinated so she popped it into the microwave for a few seconds to reheat it. "It worked."

"How was he?"

"He seemed to be okay, a lot happier than he had been before." When the coffee was done, she took a sip, wincing as she realized she had heated it a little too much. "I was right about him sending William to me; he said I was the only one he knew that he could trust."

"After all that happened, I'm not really surprised by that," Troy said as he poured a carefully measured amount of dark powder into a tube. "And considering everything he's been through, you can't really blame the guy for not trusting too many people right now."

She explained about her midnight meeting and how reluctant the dreamwalker had been to tell her where the demoness was.

"But he did tell you?"

"Yeah, he just wanted to be sure I'd be careful about who I bring with me when I go find her."

"Well, I know one thing for sure," he looked up at her. "I'm definitely going with you."

Jen nodded. "I'd figured as much." She looked down at his mess. "More explosives?"

"Yep. I decided to make these ones just a little more potent than the old ones were but the mixture's basically the same."

"That works." She took another drink of her coffee and watched as he filled the tube. While he screwed the end on to seal it, she said, "I was actually planning on talking to you about those, anyway."

"What about them?"

"He said that the demoness has a lot of traps and I figure that the best way to get past any traps a demon would set is by just plain getting rid of it."

He grinned over at her, his shaggy moustache twitching in amusement. "I knew you'd come around to my way of thinking eventually."

She shook her head and sat across the table from him. "I'm going to go down to the office in a little bit, mostly to let David know what's going on and to see if any of the rest of the team is willing to go too."

Troy nodded. "Speaking of which, I have something for you." He reached down into a box that sat on the floor next to his chair and pulled out a bullet. He slid it across the table to her. "What do you think?"

She picked it up and examined it. It looked like a normal round but it had an indentation in the nose, like a hollow point would. To her, it looked like someone had taken some of the bullet out with a very small ice cream scoop, and then etched an X across it. "What is it?"

"My latest design," he answered. "It's armor piercing, so it should work a lot better on those dark knights of yours."

Jen turned the bullet over in her hand. "Aren't most armor piercers for the rifle?"

"Not always," Troy responded. "Besides, you suck with a rifle. I just figured you'd rather have them for your pistol."

"True," Jen rolled the bullet back over to Troy. "How many of those do you have?"

"Not very many," he admitted as he tucked the round back into the box. "Only a couple hundred."

Only Troy would consider a couple hundred rounds of ammunition to be a small amount. Jen stood up and refilled her coffee cup. Rather than overheating it again, she decided to drink it as it was. "How long would it take you to make more?"

Troy looked thoughtful for a moment. "Maybe a few hours, less if I have someone come over to help me." He eyed her speculatively. "Feeling a bit impatient, are we?"

She shrugged as she headed for the door. "The longer we leave the Soul Gem with the demon, the more likely she is to be able to harness Rachel's magic." She looked back over her shoulder at him. "And I'm pretty sure we all know how ugly that would get."

"I'll make some calls and see what I can do," Troy agreed.

As Jen got dressed, she called David to let him know that she was on her way in. "I thought you'd want an update, so I figured I'd do it in person instead of just over the phone."

"Be careful," he cautioned her. "There's an icy rain coming down out here and it's already caused a few accidents. Considering the way everyone talks about your driving, I thought I'd warn you."

Jen chuckled as she got off the phone. She

looked out her window and, sure enough, there was a decent amount of sleet mixed in with the rain. She would be careful, of course, but she was amused at the idea that everyone was so concerned about her driving. She knew that to other people she seemed reckless behind the wheel but she had never actually been in an accident. The closest she had ever been to one was when she had rammed a werewolf but that could hardly have been considered accidental.

Once she was ready, she checked in on Troy. He was busily making more of his violent cocktails, so she let him be and headed out to her truck. On the way to her office, she stopped by Taco King because she simply needed an order of nachos.

When she arrived at the office, the nachos were pretty much gone. She munched on the last bites as she headed inside, nodding at Kelly, the ever-present receptionist, as she went by.

David wasn't in his office so she checked down in the basement, where the team had their meetings and trained. There, not only did she find David but the rest of the team was gathered as well. She stopped in surprise as they all looked up at her when she walked inside. "Did I forget a team briefing?" she asked as she looked around at the expectantly waiting men.

"No," Marc answered. "You were the one that called it."

Even David grinned at her confusion. "You said you had an update, so I figured it'd be easier to update everyone at the same time instead of my having to repeat it for everyone later."

Jen nodded and swallowed the last of her food. "Okay then." She stepped in front of the group. "First of all, I'm pretty sure that most of you are thinking this has to do with the black knights. It's not." She looked around the group as she asked, "Have any of you been paying any attention to the series of thefts that have been reported on the news lately?"

A couple of them nodded that they had, so she continued. "I have recently discovered that all of these thefts have been committed by the same person. He admitted to me just a few days ago that he was the one responsible and even told me what had been stolen from each place. However, he has been doing it under duress.

"His daughter, a mage named Rachel, currently resides in a Soul Gem, a device for storing massive amounts of energy. She was accidentally sucked into this item quite a while ago, so he had been carrying the Gem with him since then, looking for a way to restore her."

"Wait a minute," Mike interrupted. "Why haven't we heard about this? If something like that had happened, wouldn't people have been talking about it?"

Jen nodded. "Normally, yes. However, this happened about two hundred years ago, so to say that its old news is a bit of an understatement."

"Two hundred years ago?" J.J. asked. "How old is this guy?"

"He's a vampire, but a legal one. I already checked, and he's fully registered. But that's beside the point. What we have is an exceedingly powerful mage, trapped in a Soul Gem, which has been stolen by a demon. It's this demon that has been instructing the vampire in the thefts in return for the safekeeping of his daughter."

She paused for a moment, letting her words

sink in. Once the commotion settled, she continued. "Because of our past success in dealing with demons, it was suggested that the vampire contact us for help. He is willing to turn himself in for the crimes he's committed but not until after the Gem has been returned to him."

"Now we have to go fight another demon?" Ty asked. "Are you crazy?" He looked around at the rest of the group. "Do you all remember what happened the last time we tangled with a demon?"

"Yes, actually, I do," Marc answered. He had ended up with a broken leg over the ordeal and the cast had only been removed two days before. "But if we're talking about a demon, something needs to be done."

"None of you have to go," Jen pointed out. "Just like last time, if any of you want to help, you're more than welcome. I'm going, but none of you have to." She looked over at David as she spoke. He was the boss, after all, and she hoped she hadn't overstepped.

"She's right," David agreed. "None of you are certified to do this and honestly, I'm not sure that there even is certification for it. But none of you will be required to go and you won't be penalized for not going."

"I have a little bit of information, some helpful but some that I'm not sure how helpful it will be. The demon in this instance has been referred to many times as a demoness, so we can assume it is female. I'm not sure that it makes a difference, but it might.

"Also, we aren't even positive that this demon currently has the Soul Gem in her possession. All we know is that she is the one sending the vampire out to steal stuff in return for his daughter's safekeeping. But if she doesn't have the Gem, she will likely know where it is."

"This demon is rumored to use a lot of traps and I have been told she is highly intelligent. Because of that, she may prove more difficult than usual.

"Lastly, we have the mage in the Gem. As I said, she was quite powerful in her own right, which has only grown stronger due to the influence of the Soul Gem she's trapped in. It's believed that the demon wants her because of this power. If the demon manages to free her before we get to her, it might be able to harness her power, becoming even stronger and more dangerous."

She looked around the group as she finished speaking. "That's what I have for now."

"What about your friend?" Mike asked. "Will he be coming too?"

"Troy will, yes. I don't know about Patrick but I hope to be able to keep him out of it this time."

"So where is the furball?" J.J. asked. "Shouldn't he be here, too?"

"He's back at the house, cooking up more explosives."

David stared at her, slack-jawed. "He's making these at your house?" When she nodded, he pointed across the hall. "We have an extra room here for that kind of thing, it's reinforced concrete so that if something does go wrong, it won't drop the building on top of him."

Jen's eyes followed the direction he was indicating. "Are you sure you wouldn't mind?"

"Of course not," David answered. "Besides, if he's making these things for the team to use, we might be able to help out with some of the supplies."

"Okay, I'll let him know when I get back." She looked around the room again. There was still some murmuring, so she waited, knowing that there would be more questions.

"When are we planning on heading out?" J.J. asked.

"Probably not until later tonight at the earliest. Like I said, Troy's still making more supplies and he said he wouldn't be done for a few hours yet."

"Why don't we plan on tomorrow morning, then?" David suggested. "That way everyone can get a good night sleep and be a bit more alert in the morning." He looked at the group. "Does that sound fair?"

They all nodded, so he smiled over at Jen. "Sounds like we have a plan."

Once that was all settled, Jen headed back home. When she got there, she was surprised to see Joel's little blue minivan parked at the curb in front of her house. Curious, she parked in her driveway and headed inside.

In the kitchen, Joel and Troy had a small pile of explosives stacked on one of the counters. Jen could smell that fresh coffee had been brewed so before saying anything to either of them, she poured herself a cup. Although she and Joel had been friends for a long time, it wasn't until times like this that she remembered that he was former military, just like Troy. It made sense that he had gotten explosive training during his tour of duty as well, but in his normal daily life, it was hard to imagine him making and using bombs.

Once she had taken a couple drinks of the steaming brew, she informed Troy about the workspace that had been offered to him in the New World building.

"Awesome," he said. "With more room to work in, I can bring in some more of my equipment and this'll go a lot faster."

"And we'll be able to give you some peace and quiet, too," Joel chimed in. He stood up and stretched, almost scraping his fingertips against the ceiling as he did.

The guys gathered up the supplies and the completed explosives that they had spread across the kitchen, lugging it all out to Troy's car. "I'll follow you," Joel called to Troy when they were ready to leave.

Once they were gone, Jen settled down to relax. She briefly debated on turning on the news but after the way she had reacted last time, she thought better of it. Instead, she went into the bathroom, filled the tub with hot water and skin softening scented oils that Jaime had left for her, and settled in for a good long soak.

When she went to bed that night, neither Patrick nor Troy had returned. She wasn't overly concerned because Troy tended to lose track of time when he was working on something and Patrick had gotten into the habit of going out for a drink with the guys after work. Both of the guys had keys to her house, so she locked the front door and climbed into bed.

When she woke in the morning, both of her roommates were home. Patrick was fast asleep on his mattress but Troy was in the kitchen, frying up a batch of potatoes, eggs, peppers, and onions at the stove. He looked over at Jen as she walked in and gestured toward the coffee pot. "It's only about half an hour old so it should still be pretty hot."

She poured a cup, sniffing at the concoction on the stove. "We're supposed to be meeting up with the team this morning so we can head out after the Soul Gem. You still want to come with us?"

"Of course," Troy answered as he scooped his breakfast out onto three plates. "You weren't thinking you could leave me behind on this, were you?"

Jen shook her head. "I'm just worried, that's all. There's still a lot about this situation that we still don't know."

He handed her a plate. "For now, worry about breakfast. After we eat, we can head out and take care of business."

Jen sat at the table with her plate and watched as Troy did the same with his. Curious, she asked, "What's the other plate for?" She didn't have to look behind her to know that Patrick was still fast asleep, his snores echoed through the house.

"It'd better be for me," Joel said as he walked into the kitchen and picked up the plate. "Because I'm eating it."

Troy snickered. "The guys came down and told us that we were leaving in the morning. Since Patrick's going to be working and can't come on this one, Joel agreed to come with and help out."

"More like insisted," Joel said as he took his seat. "Troy and Marc both tried to talk me out of it but if you think you're leaving me behind again, you're crazy."

Jen shook her head. "No, you're not going. All of us on the team have been training for a while now and Troy has had much more recent military training than you have. You aren't ready for something like this."

"You can argue as much as you want," Joel said, "but I'm coming with. Troy and I got all of my gear last night, so I'm good to go."

"You're helping him?" Jen turned to Troy. "What's wrong with you?"

"Hey, either I helped him get some gear or he was going to come in jeans. Which would you have preferred?"

"Sahara's going to kill us both," she looked at Joel. "I hope you're aware of that."

He shook his head. "She already knows. I talked it over with her this morning."

Jen looked at him in shock. "She actually agreed to this insanity?"

"Look," Joel put his fork down. "You're her best friend and one of my closest friends, too. Neither of us wants to see you get hurt and believe me, if something happens while we're out there, I'll be able to hold my own." He took another bite of his potatoes. "Besides, I'm a hybrid, remember? How much do you think it's gonna take for anything to get past me to get to you?" He pointed with his fork over at Troy. "Him and me, we're a wall. Get it?"

Jen sighed, knowing that she had lost the argument before it had even started. "What type of gear did you get?"

"Same as Patrick has," Troy explained. "I just took Joel to the same place I went to and got him everything there." He looked thoughtful for a moment. "Except the rifle," he amended. "I already had that."

"You have body armor?" Jen looked over at Joel, who nodded in agreement. "And a rifle, I guess. What about a pistol for close-up?"

"We got that covered, too." Troy grinned. "He's almost as bad with one as you are but he's got one, at least."

"Hey, I'm not that bad," Joel protested.

"I said almost," Troy quipped, ducking before Jen threw her fork at him.

Once they were finished eating, Jen, Troy, and Joel headed out. Rather than taking all three vehicles, Joel opted to ride with Troy. They headed for the office and Jen prayed the entire trip that taking Joel wouldn't turn out to be a huge mistake. Much as she loved him, he was one of her closest friends after all, she didn't want him to get hurt trying to protect her. If not for her own sake, he had a wife and kids to think about. They would be devastated if anything happened to him.

When they got to the office, Jen led them inside. The rest of the team was already gathered downstairs and they were visibly surprised that Joel was there, too. "I thought it was just going to be us," Ty piped up.

"I'm surprised you're here," Jen answered. "From the sound of things yesterday, I'd figured you were staying behind on this one."

"What, and let you guys get all the glory?" Ty snickered. "No, seriously, I may not like what we're up against but we're a team so I'm here whenever you need me."

Jen smiled at him in appreciation. Ty had been the last person to warm up to her and she knew that things had been rough for a while but she was glad to find out that he would still be there for her.

"Okay, if everyone's here, let's get geared up, shall we?" Marc spoke up. He looked down at Jen. "Since Patrick's not here now, I assume he's not coming?"

Jen shook her head. "He was still sleeping when I left. I don't want him in the middle of anything more right now. He's already gotten into the middle of too much."

Marc nodded and picked up his gear bag. "Okay, then. I'll see you in a few." He headed off to the locker room to get changed.

Troy and Joel followed him into the locker room. Jen, who had gotten into her gear before leaving the house, waited for everyone to return. When the elevator bell dinged, she looked up to see David walking towards her. She stood up to greet him.

"How are you doing?" he asked once he was close. "Seems like all of this has been pretty rough on you."

Jen shrugged. "I don't like putting other people in danger but other than that, I'm okay."

David nodded. "I have to admit, I'm surprised by you. When I first brought you into the company, there were a lot of people who were questioning my decision. But you've shown some of the best instincts I've seen in a long time and now I'm starting to wonder just how far you'll be able to take that." He looked over at her as he took a seat on a bench. "It's a rare talent you have, I hope you understand that."

"Which talent?" she asked. "Getting myself into trouble or surviving it?"

He chuckled. "You seem to see things differently than everyone else does. Like with the black knights, everyone else was sure that they were a one-time deal but you were so sure that they weren't gone, it even made me wonder if you could be right."

"And then I was," she said. "That couldn't have gone over well."

David shook his head. "I heard a few people asking questions, wondering if there was a special reason that you knew they weren't gone.

I'm still not sure that all of them believed me when I said you're just good like that."

Jen shrugged. "It just seemed too easy, that's all."

"But that wasn't the only time you've done something like that. When the reports were all over the news about the thefts, I think you were the only person who recognized that they were all connected. That's not something we can teach, that's all you. Like I said, you've got some good instincts."

"Thanks, I guess," Jen answered. "But I'm not sure how I'm supposed to be proud of something that I don't have any control over."

David sighed. "Just accept the praise, would you? Besides, there was a point I was getting to with that."

"Okay, thank you for the compliments. What was your point?"

David laughed fully that time. "And so very direct, too. That makes things a lot easier when you don't have to dance in circles.

"Whenever I make an inquiry to the NPIB, they require a full report on why I want the information. Since most of those inquiries have been because of you requesting information, your name has been on a lot of the reports. There are a few people in the NPIB who are starting to look more closely at you."

While Jen realized that all of the response teams ultimately answered to the NPIB, she hadn't expected to be so personally involved in any of the Board's matters. With David's statement, she wondered whether getting their attention like that was a good thing or a bad thing. She blinked over at David, unsure of how to respond. "Have I done something wrong? Am I in trouble over this?"

"No," he shook his head. "But don't be surprised if agents want to come out to talk with you soon. I think they're finally starting to be as impressed with you as I am."

Jen was confused. "So why do they want to talk to me? I've told you everything I know about all this already."

"I know that," he said, "but I think they have bigger plans for you." Noticing that she was still confused, he sighed. "Look, I don't want to lose you, I hope you know that. But the NPIB tends to snap up talent wherever they find it. I just want you to remember that you have friends back here once you move on to better pastures."

Finally, a light turned on in Jen's head. "You think they're going to offer me a job?"

David nodded. "I already gave them a great recommendation for you." He smiled at her. "It'd be nice to have someone on the inside, finally. And this is a great opportunity for you."

Jen sat in silence, stunned. She hadn't been working for New World for very long at all and the last thing she had expected was for the NPIB to be looking into her, let alone recruiting her. If anything, she wouldn't expect to hear of someone moving from a response team to NPIB until they had much more time in grade than she had earned. "But what about you guys? What about the team? I can't just leave you guys like this."

"We can always hire someone else. Granted, they won't be you, but we'll be okay."

Any further discussion they might have had on the subject was delayed as Troy, Joel, Ty, Marc, and J.J. walked back into the briefing room. Marc and J.J. stopped when they saw David but Joel grinned and waved. "So how do I look?"

"Like someone playing dress-up," Jen retorted. Joel was wearing black pants with pockets down both legs and a matching black shirt. His belt now held a holster and Jen wasn't sure she wanted to know what kind of pistol it held.

Once everyone was assembled, Jen looked at the group. "Okay, last chance to change your minds." Nobody took her up on the offer so as a group they headed for the elevator. Again, Jen had no option but to ride with someone else but instead of riding with J.J. as she usually would, she chose to ride with Marc. As unit leader, he was usually in the lead truck when they went anywhere so she figured it would be better if she rode with him, considering she was the only one who knew where they were going.

A gentle rain had started to fall while they were inside the building but the dark cloud overhead promised worse weather to come. As they headed out of town, Jen eyed the clouds suspiciously. Even though she didn't believe that they were paranormal in origin, she wasn't willing to dismiss anything out of hand. But as she pointed the way, following the dreamwalker's directions, she discovered that the clouds weren't centered over where they were headed after all. She wasn't sure why she was relieved by this, but she was.

The rain steadily got worse as they drove until it was coming down hard and fast enough that they had to slow down. The windshield wipers simply didn't move the water out of the way fast enough. Finally, they were forced to turn off the highway and onto surface streets because the traffic on the highway was too dangerous. Jen squinted through the water, no longer as sure that she would be able to find the right place without following the directions she had been given.

After only a half hour, some of the scenery they passed started to seem recognizable and Jen felt the familiar tingle down her spine that told her she was on the right track. She pointed to a four-way-stop. "Turn left here."

Marc didn't question her directions, trusting in her judgment. They turned left, followed by the rest of the team. Soon, more started to look familiar and Jen recognized that they were back on the path they would have taken, had they continued to follow the highway. She led them further into a high-end, ritzy neighborhood of town. At one intersection Jen stopped, uncertain if they were still in the right area. It felt right, but it looked like far too expensive of an area to be inhabited by demons.

Finally, she decided to trust in both the dreamwalker's directions and the tingle she still felt. Neither of them had led her wrong before so she just had to have a little faith now.

The houses grew further and further apart as they left the city limits until there was almost a minute worth of driving in between each property. One day, she mused to herself, she would like to have a place as nice as these ones were. For now, she would just be happy with the new place she just bought.

She had them stop in front of an enormous gated piece of land, well outside of town. The lawns were manicured and clean, making Jen wonder if this was the right place. She looked around the rest of the team and their expressions clearly showed that they had doubts, too. "I think we're here," she said to Marc.

Marc looked at the property that they were stopped in front of, dubiousness etched into his features. "Are you sure?"

Jen shook her head. "I think it's the place that we are heading to but something doesn't feel right."

He nodded. "We might as well have a look, then." He parked the truck off the side of the road and stepped out.

The dark clouds that Jen had noticed earlier had moved closer, blocking out much of the sun's light and bathing everything in a dim haze. The rain didn't help, either. It had let up a little bit and was now more of a thin sprinkle than the torrential downfall that it had been closer into town. As Marc and Jen stepped across the street to evaluate the area behind the gate, the rest of the team parked behind their truck and followed suit.

They started to gather outside the front gate but Marc stopped them. "We should probably stay out of view," he explained. "If there's anyone watching, they'll know we're here immediately if we just stand there." Instead, he led everyone off to the side where they could walk around the perimeter and, in a few places, look over the stone wall to see the area beyond. "This way, we should be able to maintain the element of surprise," he explained.

It was by far the largest piece of property that they had seen yet, even in this area where land was measured in acreage. "You know, we could probably fit half of downtown in there," Troy pointed out. Nobody disagreed.

Before they had even made it halfway around the fence line, Marc stopped. "This goes a lot further than I had expected," he pointed out. "Maybe it'd be better if we just found a way in somewhere along the fence line over here." Because of the sheer size of the property, the suggestion made sense but Jen suspected that it also had to do with the amount of pain she was sure Marc was in. His cast had only been off for a couple of days and he still wasn't quite up to normal strength yet, although he would never admit it. Even though she had noticed the slight limp that he had developed as they were walking, Jen didn't want to call him on it and put him on the defensive. She just hoped that if he felt badly enough, he would fall back and let the rest of the group do the heavy lifting.

They walked further along the fence until they found a section that had trees growing close on their side of the wall. Some of the branches hung over to the other side and Ty pointed out, "That's probably the best place for us to go over that I've seen yet."

All of them agreed, so one by one they hauled themselves over the fence. Once everyone was gathered on the other side of the wall, they headed across the greenery, hoping that they were headed for whatever house was in the middle of the sprawling lawn. Over a minute of travel further, they saw the first buildings.

Rather than discovering the single house they had expected, they found a small handful of buildings, each of which were connected through covered walkways and closed-in corridors. The main house, while huge, was quite pleasant looking and Jen again questioned whether they were in the right place. "Seems too nice to be a demon's house."

Troy agreed. "Are you sure this is the right place?"

"I think so," Jen shrugged. "This is where I was told, but it doesn't seem..."

She stopped, and the rest of the team stopped to see why she had stopped talking. As she pointed to the ground, everyone else gathered around to see what she was looking at. A scattering of large hoof prints was embedded in the mud.

"The demon has a horse?" Joel asked. "What kind of weird demon rides a horse?"

"Probably not the type of horse you're thinking of," Mike said. "Look at how big these are and how deep they're sunk into the ground. That's a damn big horse and it's carrying a lot of weight, too."

"Okay, so these are really big horses, then." Joel looked around at the team. "Don't all rich people invest in horses?"

Jen and J.J. exchanged glances. Neither one had to say anything; they could tell that both of them believed that these prints were likely made by the mounts of the dark-armored knights.

After all, normal horse hooves weren't cloven.

They continued on towards the house, keeping a watchful eye for any more signs of the gigantic knights. They moved quickly and carefully towards their destination until the baying of hounds sounded across the grounds.

"Oh, shit," Mike swore as the beasts leapt into view. "It's them."

"Whoa," breathed Joel as the monstrous dogs came closer. "Those things are huge!"

"Yeah," responded Troy as he grinned over at his friend. "But we're bigger."

"Yeah," Joel agreed. He giggled, an oddly high-pitched noise to come from such a large man, as he and Troy stepped forward to meet the beasts.

Troy took a knee, leveling his rifle at the closest hellhound. The great dog slowed, its momentum disrupted by the torrent of bullets that assaulted it. When the beast finally stopped, he called over to Joel, "Now!"

Joel leapt into the fray and swung up towards the dog's throat with a logging axe that Jen hadn't been aware he was carrying. With one powerful strike, he buried the head of the weapon deep into the savage beast's neck, almost severing its head in the process. As he wrenched the enormous axe back out of the dog's throat, it fell, motionless.

"It's a dog-eat-dog world, you know," Troy commented as he turned his attention to the other hound.

Jen and the rest of the team prepared to tear into the second dog, only to find Troy blocking their line of fire as he slammed another clip into his rifle. He opened fire on the second hellhound with every bit as much enthusiasm as he had shown with the first. The dog howled in pain as the bullets stopped its charge.

Joel was quick to pick up on the idea and as soon as Troy stopped firing, he swung down with all his strength, driving his axe into the back of the creature's head. The force of the blow drove the beast's muzzle the ground, muffling its dying cries.

The pair of hybrids exchanged thumbs-up signs and grins as Troy settled another magazine into his rifle and pocketed the expended ones.

Their excitement was short lived, however, as a pair of large creatures galloped into view.

The mounted knights, armor slick and gleaming in the light rain, charged at the group. One of the knights drew an enormous sword as he rode, swinging it at the team as he tore through them.

Troy grabbed Joel and threw him to the side before leaping out of the path of the sweeping blade himself. He opened fire as soon as he landed, spraying bullets into the armor-plated flank of the horse.

Jen dodged as well, quickly sidestepping until she was behind J.J. and out of the red-crested knight's path. Marc tried to run with her but tripped and fell to the ground, barely rolling out from in front of the mount's hooves. The knight turned its attention to J.J. and Jen, drawing its own massive sword as it approached them.

Ty tried to move away from the blue-crested knight but he wasn't able to move quickly enough. Mike yanked him off his feet, barely pulling him out of the way of the knight's sweeping blade. As soon as Ty regained his footing, he and Mike opened fire on the knight, adding their ammunition to the storm of bullets that Troy continued to rain down on the beast. The knight turned to trample the prone hybrids, rearing up to slam down on top of them.

As Troy's pistol clicked, signaling that his clip was empty, he dropped his back to the ground. At the same time, Joel rolled up to a knee and buried his axe in the horse's chest. Already prone, Troy rolled out of the way as the mount and its rider came crashing to the ground. Troy scrambled to his feet and backed away from the beasts but Joel was trapped beneath the immense horse creature. It was obvious that Joel was still alive under the horse because even from where she was, Jen could hear him growling.

With the red-crested knight in front of himself and Jen, sword raised high to cleave through the pair of them, J.J. ripped one of Troy's custom-built magnetic explosives from his belt and threw it at the knight. It stuck to the knight's armor on the side of its ribcage, just below the arm. The blast knocked the knight from its mount and it struggled to regain its footing.

As it tried to stand, Mike ran up behind it and, following J.J.'s example, stuck another grenade to its back. The second explosion caused the knight to overbalance and it fell forward, stumbling against its mount as it tried to keep its footing.

As the knight stumbled around, Troy threw a grenade of his own at the blue-crested knight, dropping that one to a knee as well. Marc, who finally managed to climb to his feet, ran forward and tugged at the knight's helmet, burying his fingers in the blue hair of its crest and tugging as hard as he could. Troy stepped forward and kicked the knight's foot, knocking it further off balance. Once Marc was able to pull the knight's helmet free, revealing a blackened mass of hairless flesh, Troy jumped onto its back and emptied his pistol into the back of the creature's head.

While J.J. pulled another grenade off his belt, the red-crested knight's mount turned toward him, fangs bared as it moved to take a bite out of him. "Oh, hell no!" J.J. said as he shoved the grenade against the bridle at the base of the horse-creature's neck. He turned and pounced on Jen, smashing her to the ground and covering her body with his as the explosion rolled over them.

"Next time," she grunted as she pushed him off of her, "buy me dinner first." She pulled her shotgun up and blasted both barrels into the creature's neck, miraculously striking it in the same area as where the blast had just shredded its skin.

She dropped the weapon as she saw Ty and Mike, running for the last remaining knight. They rammed into the giant's back, slamming it into the ground and barely missing Jen and J.J.

Once they had it on the ground, Ty and Mike drew their pistols and pressed them into the small open spaces in the knight's armor. They fired every round they had already loaded into their weapons and finally the creature stopped moving.

# Chapter 13

"So much for the element of surprise," Troy said as he helped to pull Joel free from the horse's body. "I'm pretty sure that if they hadn't already known we're coming, they do now."

Everyone else agreed, so they stepped up their pace and headed directly for the main building, giving up any pretense of subterfuge. They were almost jogging by the time they arrived, not stopping until they reached the ground in front of the steps leading up to the front porch. There they checked their weapons to be sure that they were ready. As soon as they all nodded that they were ready, Marc reached out and opened the door.

He quickly stepped into a large foyer, followed quickly by the rest of the group. The room was spacious, with lush carpeting underfoot and illuminated by a soft glow from the chandelier overhead. Stained glass windows lined the walls, with rich tapestries hanging between them. Low wooden tables stood under each of the windows, each of which held a decorative knickknack. One held a bronze statue of a bird, another held a large, star-shaped crystal, another held a decorative blue glass vase with a branch of a blooming cherry tree in it.

"I see you made it past my guardians," a husky, feminine voice spoke to them. At the far end of the room, a large flight of marble stairs covered in rich velvet carpeting climbed to the next floor. The most beautiful woman Jen had ever seen stood two steps from the top, one hand resting on the dark wooden banister. She was tall and slender, not unlike Jen but with a lot more curves to her body. Her long auburn hair floated around her shoulders in soft waves and her floor-length red velvet dress was cut low enough to show her navel.

As everyone looked up at her, she raised her other hand to her lips and blew a kiss out over them. Her lips curved into a sly smile, and the tingle in Jen's lower spine warned her that there was something seriously wrong. The men stood all around her, stunned by the woman's presence. None of them moved, seemingly happy to just stand and bask in her presence.

"Where is the Soul Gem?" Jen asked the woman.

She only smiled in return. "I know that isn't what you really want." She stepped down a couple more stairs. "Come, join me and you can see all of your dreams fulfilled."

"Not a chance," Jen retorted. Troy, J.J., and Mike stepped towards the stairs, as though they were sleepwalking. Jen looked over at them in shock. "What are you doing?"

"They are about to see the answer to all of their fantasies," the woman purred. "Why don't you join them?"

Jen shook her head. "I'll kill you before that. Now, where is the Gem?"

The woman laughed. "You can't possibly kill me; don't you understand that? The worst you could possibly do to me is to send me back to Derathim and I would simply come back and kill you and all your friends if you were to try."

She arched a perfectly shaped eyebrow at the statement.

"Figures," Jen muttered as she shook the men. None of them even seemed to notice, until she reached out and slapped Troy across the face. "Snap out of it, will you?"

He blinked at her in confusion. "What the hell was that?"

Before she could answer, Jen knew that the demoness had control of him again as his eyes went blank. She also knew that she was in real trouble this time; with all of the men out of action, she wasn't sure she could take on a demon by herself. If she couldn't figure out a way to snap them all out of the trance the demon had them in, she knew that there was a good chance that none of them may survive it.

"All I can do is send you back where you came, hmm?" Jen looked up at the demoness again and nodded slowly. "Sounds like a deal." She ran towards the stairs, intent on stopping the demon any way she could but before she was able to take more than two steps, she was stopped as Troy reached out and took hold of her.

"You've got to be kidding me," she said as she looked down at Troy's lifeless eyes. She struggled but knew there was no point in resisting. Troy was a hybrid, far stronger than she.

The demoness stepped slowly down the stairs, trailing her fingertips along the banister as she walked. When she reached the carpeted area on the floor, she looked at the group. "Follow me," she instructed them.

She led them down a hall in the back of the room. At the end of the hall, she opened a heavy wooden door and stepped inside. There, the carpeting ended and the floor returned to hard, bare stone. The heavy tapestries continued to decorate the walls but the floor space was dominated by a large table made out of a single block of yellow stone that was stained brown across the top side. "Put her on the table," she said as Troy dragged Jen into the room.

Troy pulled her over to the table, despite her protests. J.J. stepped forward to help lift her onto the rough stone surface and he held her feet as Troy held her arms.

Jen tried to kick and squirm, doing her best

to wrench out of their grasp but they barely seemed to notice.

"You will serve nicely to please my master," the demoness said as she picked up an ornately carved wooden box. She opened it and pulled out a smooth black dagger that shone like glass in the dim light. Somehow, Jen knew that it was the sacrificial dagger that William had stolen from the museum. Realizing the danger she was in, Jen struggled against her captives more strenuously but they held tight.

The demoness examined the blade of the knife for a moment before she turned and handed it, handle-first, to Joel. "Remove her heart," she instructed him.

"Joel, what are you doing?" Jen pled with her friend as he turned towards her. "Snap out of this, come on!"

Heedless of her cries, Joel stepped to the edge of the altar. He looked down at her with eyes as soulless as Troy's had been and raised the dagger above his head.

Jen screamed, hoping to wake him from the trance the demoness had put him under. She kicked out at the same time, managing to free one of her feet from J.J.'s grasp. She kicked out again, this time catching J.J. in the face with the toe of her boot. She didn't care how much damage she did to him; she would apologize for that later. For now, she just needed to wake him up before she was killed.

J.J. stepped back, letting go of her foot and blinking in shock, raising a hand to his bloody nose. "What the hell?" he asked.

Not wanting to waste time with explanation, Jen flipped herself away from Joel, barely moving out of the way as the blade came down and slammed into the table where she had been lying only a second before. Jen screeched again as he lifted the dagger again, preparing for another strike.

J.J. reached out for Jen and she realized that he was already fully under the demoness's thrall once again. She kicked at him and at the rest of the team who were gathered around the table, watching. She hoped to connect with another one, maybe even doing enough damage to wake them up for more than just a couple of seconds, but the demoness quickly thwarted that idea.

"Take her," she called out. "Hold her down so that she can no longer move."

Before she was even finished speaking, more people grabbed hold of Jen, pinning her to the table once more. She struggled against them, screaming, but she knew that she had no chance. She couldn't get away.

As her team moved to hold her more securely, they moved around the table, holding and releasing her in turn as they moved. When Jen saw a chance, she jerked her body as hard as she could, kicking out in two directions, punching in two more, and even resorting to biting one of them. The tactic worked, because enough of them let go at once to allow her to buck off the table.

She dropped to the floor and launched at the evil woman, determined to reach her before she could try to kill her again. Hands reached out to her as she moved but they moved slowly in their dream-like state and she wasn't about to slow down for them. She swung with all her fear-fueled might as she approached the demoness and landed a solid punch to her face.

The demon screamed at the blow and the

men were able to shake off her spell. They all looked around in shock, trying to figure out what had happened and where they were. Their clarity only lasted for a moment, however, as the demoness took hold of them again.

She wiped a thin stream of black blood from the side of her mouth. "Take her," she said as she looked at the smear on her pale hand.

Jen howled again as her team grabbed her. "NO! Wake up, come on, don't do this!" she cried, but her pleas fell on deaf ears, just as they had before. Tears flowed down her face as she begged her teammates to wake up.

"You are much stronger of spirit than I had expected," the demon said as she looked back over at Jen again. "I have a much better idea for you than just a simple sacrifice."

She called out in a language that Jen didn't recognize. One of the tapestries moved, revealing yet another passage behind it. A man stepped from the tunnel that had been hidden behind the tapestry and looked over at the demoness.

The demon smiled and pointed to Jen, still talking in her strange language. The man looked at Jen appraisingly as she spoke and, once she was finished talking, he stepped closer to the captive.

He was taller than Jen, with light brown hair that was streaked with dark blond. He wasn't wearing a shirt, which just accentuated his muscular chest and slim waist. His eyes were a warm brown color, but almost as expressionless as Jen's team's were.

He reached out and ran a hand over her, examining her face, her hair, and the rest of her body. Finally, he looked back at the demoness and nodded.

The demoness's lips curved into a tight, thin-lipped, humorless smile as the man reached out again and took Jen by an arm. His grip was like iron, holding her even more strongly than Troy had. The demoness ordered the men to let go of Jen and as soon as they released her, the newcomer held a hand out between himself and the demoness. He drew a circle in the air with his hand, which turned into a shimmering circle of green and purple light. He stepped into the magical circle, dragging Jen with him.

As soon as the pair was inside, the circle shrank and faded from view.

The moment Jen disappeared through the magical circle, both hybrids began to violently shake. Joel was the first to come out of the demoness's spell and when he stepped forward towards the evil woman, her sneer turned to a gasp of surprise. She started to speak, but he was on her immediately. He grabbed her by the throat, fingertips digging into her pale skin, and hoisted her into the air, shaking her roughly. "Where is she? Where is she?" he demanded, over and over again.

Troy took a moment longer to break her thrall but he broke free much more dramatically. A growl began low in his throat and his knuckles whitened as his hands clenched tightly. The growl turned to a bellow as he dropped to his knees, slamming both fists onto the stone floor. Blood spurted from both of his fists, further bringing him out of her spell.

Even as Joel shook her, the demoness looked back and forth between the hybrids, not sure which was more dangerous. When Troy launched through the air at her, Joel let go, leaving her suspended off the floor for a millisecond before Troy reached her.

Troy slammed her against a wall forcefully enough to crack the skull of an ordinary human. He dug his thick, sharp fingernails into the side of her face. "Do your tricks still work if you aren't pretty?" he growled at her as he tugged at the skin of her face.

Her power over the rest of the group gone, the team began to come out of their stupor. While the hybrids had the demon occupied, the humans looked around in wonder.

Marc was the first to truly come to his senses. He stepped closer to Troy and put a hand on the furious hybrid's shoulder. "Don't kill her."

"Why not?" Troy asked without taking his eyes or claws from the woman. "She tried to kill Jen." His voice was barely comprehensible through the growing that had not yet stopped emanating from his throat.

"I know," Marc agreed. "But she's the only one who knows where Jen is. If you kill her, we might not be able to find out where she's gone."

"Can I hurt her?" his eyes narrowed into slits at the question.

"Maybe later. For now, I think we need to keep her here, alive." He looked back at the rest of the group. "Search the house. Jen might still be in here somewhere and I don't care how many walls you need to knock down, I want to be sure before we leave."

Everyone nodded and headed out, knowing to keep within eyesight of each other without having to be reminded. The first place that Ty looked was behind the tapestry where the second demon had appeared but there was nothing but bare wall hidden behind it. He pressed on the stones, looking for a hidden passage, but wasn't able to find anything. The rest of the walls and the floor in that room were searched just as thoroughly, but none of the team found anything. Once they were done there, they moved out to search the rest of the house.

When they finished searching it and were satisfied that Jen was nowhere on the premises, Marc sent J.J. and Mike out to grab one of the vehicles. "Ram the gate if you have to but I want those rigs here where we can get to them."

He looked back over at the hybrids who were still standing guard over the demoness. "I don't want to have to deal with any more of this bitch's tricks."

Jen will return in Beautiful Monsters.

Available February, 2024

Shanon L. Mayer is the author of multiple book series, including the Chronicles of the Chosen, the Inland Sea series and the Jen Rice series.

She was born in Portland, Oregon in 1978 and lived most of her life in the Pacific Northwest. She received a Bachelor of Arts in Business Administration from Washington State University in 2013, which did nothing to quench her passion for the fantasy genre.

www.ingramcontent.com/pod-product-compliance
Lightning Source LLC
Chambersburg PA
CBHW030345200726
48286CB00013B/299